# LIFEBOAT 12

# LIFEBOAT 12

## SUSAN HOOD

Based on a true story

Simon & Schuster Books for Young Readers

NEW YORK   LONDON   TORONTO   SYDNEY   NEW DELHI

SIMON & SCHUSTER BOOKS FOR YOUNG READERS
An imprint of Simon & Schuster Children's Publishing Division
1230 Avenue of the Americas, New York, New York 10020
Text copyright © 2018 by Susan Hood
Jacket illustration copyright © 2018 by Mike Heath
SIMON & SCHUSTER BOOKS FOR YOUNG READERS is a trademark of
Simon & Schuster, Inc.
For information about special discounts for bulk purchases, please contact Simon & Schuster
Special Sales at 1-866-506-1949 or business@simonandschuster.com.
The Simon & Schuster Speakers Bureau can bring authors to your live event. For more
information or to book an event, contact the Simon & Schuster Speakers Bureau
at 1-866-248-3049 or visit our website at www.simonspeakers.com.
Book design by Greg Stadnyk
Map illustration copyright © Thinkstock
The text for this book was set in Sabon.
Manufactured in the United States of America
0918 FFG
First Edition
2  4  6  8  10  9  7  5  3  1
Library of Congress Cataloging-in-Publication Data
Names: Hood, Susan, author.
Title: Lifeboat 12 / Susan Hood.
Other titles: Lifeboat twelve
Description: First edition. | New York : Simon & Schuster Books for Young Readers, [2018]
| Summary: In 1940, a group of British children, their escorts, and some sailors struggle to
survive in a lifeboat when the ship taking them to safety in Canada is torpedoed.
Includes historical notes.
Identifiers: LCCN 2017034872| ISBN 9781481468831 (hardcover : alk. paper)
| ISBN 9781481468855 (eBook)
Subjects: | CYAC: Novels in verse. | Survival—Fiction. | World War, 1939–1945—Evacuation
of civilians—Great Britain--Fiction. | World War, 1939–1945—Children—Fiction. | Ocean
travel—Fiction. | Ocean liners—Fiction. | Lifeboats—Fiction.
Classification: LCC PZ7.5.H665 Lif 2018 | DDC [Fic]—dc23
LC record available at https://lccn.loc.gov/2017034872

For Ken Sparks,
with thanks to my mother-in-law, Nancy Hurst-Brown,
a British evacuee whose childhood letters home led me to
this story

# ESCAPE

# SUMMER, 1940

## The Envelope

I shouldn't do it.
I know I shouldn't.

I'll be in trouble
if I open the large envelope
addressed to my parents.

But it's stamped
"on His Majesty's Service."
It's not every day
a family like mine
gets a letter from the King.

The clock tick, tick, ticks.

I glance down the hall
to make sure I'm alone.
I slide my finger
under the flap,
and peer inside.

Dear Sir (or Madam),
I am directed by the
Children's Overseas Reception Scheme . . .
It's nothing,
a dull form letter
but . . . wait!
Someone has written in my name—
 your preliminary application
 has been considered
 by the Board and
 they have decided that
 KENNETH J. SPARKS
 is ~~are~~ suitable for being
 sent to . . . CANADA.


"What are you doing?"
cries my stepmum,
seizing the letter from my hands.
"That is not addressed to you.
Charles! Charles!
This cheeky son of yours
wants a good clout about the ears!"


"That letter is about *me*!" I say.
"You're sending me away!"


I glare up at my father
who appears in the doorway.
My stepmum got her wish—
to get rid of me.

"Ken, let me explain,"
says my dad.
                    "This letter could save your life."


## The Reasons Why

They sit me down.
I shrug their hands off my shoulders
and stare at the floor,
heart slamming,
heat rising.
They talk and talk,
voices swirling in the air
rising and falling,
overlapping, interrupting,
weaving a net,
a trap,
but I'm not going
to fall for it.

I try to block them out.
I concentrate on
slowing the storm in my head.
They're sending me away!
        But hang on,
                what's that about the Germans?

"The Germans are coming," says Dad.
"France surrendered this summer

and the Nazis are gunning
for England next.
Hundreds of thousands
of parents applied
to have their kids sent
out of harm's way."

"You're lucky
to have been selected," says Mum.
"I have a sister
in Edmonton, Canada.
You can live with her.
With your father out of work,
money is tight.
We can rent out your room
to help pay for rations."

"Just think—sailing on a ship!" says Dad.
"It will be an adventure!
You'll make your way in the world.
Get your head out of those books. . . ."

My books? My stories
of buccaneers and buried gold,
cowboys, braves and days of old. . . .

I snort.
Most parents would be chuffed
to have a kid who loves to read.

I read them because
they take me away . . .
far from the way I'm living.

My three-year-old sister toddles over
and rests her head on my knees.

I run my hand over her curls.
"What about Margaret?
Shouldn't she go, too?"

"She's too young," says Mum.
"Only ages five through fifteen are allowed."

At thirteen I'll be one of the oldest.

"No adults?" I ask.

"Parents can't go," says my dad,
"but you'll have escorts—
a whole staff of
doctors, nurses, teachers, priests
who are volunteering.
Yes, son, you're one of the lucky ones.
You leave in September.
You mustn't tell your friends," says Dad.
"Loose lips sink ships,
you know."

"And there will be a new overcoat for you,"
says Mum
as if that clinches the deal.

I squint up at her and think,
I'm as good as gone.

I tear out of the house.


## Escape

I dash
down the streets,
down the railway line,
across the tracks,
over a fence.

There in the wall,
behind the loose brick,
I snatch my stash
of penny cannon fireworks.
I stick some in a tree,
strike a match to the fuse,
and back away.
I watch as the wick
sputters,
smokes,
sparks.

*BLAM!*
It makes quite a hole.

The charcoal-scented smoke wafts away
and my fury with it.
The smoke distracts me
as it does angry bees.

Let's face it.
My stepmum has never liked me.

She calls me a terror,
a little so-and-so.
I wish my own mum
were alive.
The doctors told her
she wasn't supposed to have children,
but she didn't listen.
She died soon after I was born.

It's all my fault.

But why did my dad
have to marry my nanny?
Well, I wouldn't have Margaret otherwise. . . .
Sure, she's a bother sometimes,
but she makes me laugh.

I think about my stepmum,
the ship, and this evacuation plan.

I feel like a hand-me-down
my stepmum doesn't want,
so she'll donate me to a good cause.

Forget it. I'm not going.
She won't get rid of me that easily.

I climb over another fence,
hoist myself up a tree,
and grab an apple to eat.
She thinks I'm a terror?
Just because I like to
scrump a few apples?
My dad just says
I'm full of beans.
I can't get away with much
or I get a clout round the ear hole
or the cane at school.

Now they want to send me away
across the ocean.
Well, I'm not going.

## The New World

That's what they call it.
Wonder what it's like?
Everything I own

is old,
tired,
secondhand.
Well, I got a new mum,
but I'm her secondhand kid.
She makes me feel
worn,
torn,
worthless.

A New World
sounds wide open,
a chance to start my miserable life
over again.

A black ant
makes his way along the
gnarled branch
high off the ground.
He's brave, that one.

I chew on my apple.
How can it
taste sour and sweet
at the same time?

Maybe Dad's right. It will be an adventure . . .
far from the rations,
far from my stepmum's scowl,
far from teacher's cane,

far from the war . . .
'twould be folly to miss this chance.

They say I'm one of the lucky ones.
Maybe I am.

# A Sea Change

A dog starts barking.
A man yells,
"Hey! You again?
Get down out of that tree.
Clear off or
I'll have your hide!"
I pluck another apple,
jump down, and run
for the fence,
the dog at my heels.
Up and over, I make my getaway.

All the way home
I think of narrow escapes
and high adventure.
Okay, I'll show them!

I'll go and grow up
like the chaps in my books—
like Wart and Robin Hood.

I'll go to sea like Jim Hawkins or Robinson Crusoe.

How long will I be gone?
Months?
Years?
                    Will I ever come back?


## Liver Again

"Oh, you're home now, are you?"
says my stepmum,
as I walk in the door.
"You get a little hungry
and all is forgiven."

"Leave him be, Nora," says my dad.
"He's had a lot to think about.
Come on, son, let's sit down to eat."

Mum places a plate
of roly-poly on the table.
I've watched her make it before—
a bit of chopped liver
rolled up in a pastry
of flour, oatmeal, and suet.
Disgusting.
I grab a potato and say,
"I'm not hungry."

"You will be if this rationing
gets any worse," says Mum.
"Those Huns keep sinking
our food supply ships
and you'll be lucky
for any scrap you get.
That's almost the last meat for the week,
so eat up."

"Any sweets, Mummy?"
asks Margaret.
"Yes, dear," says Mum.
"A nice baked milk pudding
for dessert.
Now eat your roly-poly."

*Oof,* I'm ready to get out of here.

## Something New

I haven't had store-bought clothes
in months . . . years maybe.
"Make do and mend,"
everyone says,
part of the war effort.

I wear hand-me-downs
from cousins and neighbors,
patched, faded, worn, torn,

with stains that won't come out,
with arms too long,
legs too short.

But it's cold in Canada,
says my stepmum.
With no overcoats
to be found from friends,
I find myself fussed over
in a shop of secondhand clothes.

"Here's just the ticket, young man,"
says the storekeeper,
who seems beside himself
to have a customer.
"Try it on."

I look in the mirror
and run my hands
down the good English wool—
dark gray,
double-breasted,
with wide lapels
deep pockets and a belt.
I don't recognize the person
smiling back at me in the mirror.
He almost looks like a man.
A man with money.

"Is it warm?" asks my stepmum.
"That's the important thing."

"Oh yes," I say.

Mum asks the storekeeper,
"What's the cost?"

"Fifteen shillings, Madam."

"Fifteen! Fifteen shillings
of our hard-earned money?"

I knew it.
Nearly a pound sterling on me?
That'll never happen.
I start to untie the belt.

"Oh, very well," she says.
"There's no getting round it.
I hope you appreciate
all we're doing for you, Ken."

"Yes, Mum.
Thank you, Mum."

I follow her out
with a grin on my face.
This coat is probably the nicest thing
I've ever owned.

## It Begins

September sneaks up on me.
I'll be leaving soon.
Mum is making me clean out my room
to ready it for a boarder.
I admit it's a bloomin' mess,
but I like it that way.
I stack my comics
and shove them under the bed.
*Oof,* it's hot, even though the sun
is starting to go down.

I sweep some trash into the dust bin
when . . . what's that?
Sirens.
We've heard them before.
It's probably just another drill.
Then come the explosions—
*BOOM!*

# BOOM!

# BOOM!

"Dad!" I call.
"Mum?"

The bombs are not far off—
blasts shatter the air.
The earth shudders.
Margaret wails.
I hear Mum's footsteps rushing to her side.
"Dad!" I yell. "DAD!"

"You hold your noise, you!" says Mum.
"You're frightening Margaret!"

"No more Phoney War," says my dad.
"We're in the thick of it now."

"What should we do?
Should we get to the shelter?"

"No, c'mon," Dad says. "Get under the table.
If it's going to hit us, it's going to hit us."

The four of us
spend the night
huddled
under the table.
Blasts flash in the dark,

momentarily exposing
the fear on our faces
as the table jumps
and the cutlery rattles.
Teacups clatter off the shelves
and crash to the floor.

Margaret fusses and cries,
but finally falls off to sleep,
overcome and wrung out.
I hunker down,
and stare at the floor,
sleepless, in shock.
This is it.
Hitler has taken over Europe.
And now he's coming for England.
He's coming for us.

# SUNDAY, 8 SEPTEMBER

## Fallout

At first light,
Dad, Mum, and I stagger to
the wireless to hear what happened.
The news makes me dizzy
as reporters reel off numbers—
more than three hundred bombers,
six hundred escort fighter planes,
daylight raiders,
sparking sky-high firestorms
that lit the way
for a second wave of
three hundred night bombers—
more than three hundred tons of bombs
dropped on London last night.

Our buses, factories,
and power stations have been hit,
hospitals attacked,
houses smashed.
They call it the *Blitz*.
"Dad, what does it mean?" I ask.

"Short for *blitzkrieg*," he says,
"German for 'lightning war.' "

Dad and I go up to London
to see for ourselves.
Dazed people
pick their way
through piles of rubble,
past a three-story house
with the front walls blown off.
Most of the rooms and furniture are intact,
but exposed to the street,
like a life-size version of Margaret's dollhouse.
At the corner,
headlines shout the news:
100s DEAD!
MORE THAN 1000 HURT!
1000s HOMELESS IN ONE DAY!

Everywhere we look
there's smoke, ash,
glittering glass,
anger, confusion.
Fire engines pump water
from the Thames,
but red-hot fires rise
and reflect off the clouds,
so it seems
there's nowhere safe.
The world is coming apart.

We think of the London Zoo.
"Dad, the animals!"
"Don't worry," Dad says.
"Most were sent north a year ago.
They killed the snakes
and other poisonous reptiles
so the bombs
wouldn't set them free."
I shudder to think
of snakes slithering out.
But now
a new danger
hisses from the air.

"Look at this, Dad,"
I say, pointing to
a gray, jagged metal bit
in the street.
"Shrapnel," says Dad.
"It's a piece from an exploded bomb."

"Can I touch it?"
"Yes, it won't hurt you now."
I pick up the twisted metal shard
and pocket it—
a memento of the day,
of London in pieces;
a reminder of how lucky I am
to be whole, to be alive.

We hurry home.
And tonight
it begins again.

## S Is for Shelter

Night two.
Wailing
air raid sirens
rattle our sleep
rising, falling,
rising, falling,

"Get up, Ken," says my dad.
"Don't forget your gas mask.
Hurry!"

"Where are we going?"

"To the shelter down the street," says Dad.
"It's not safe at home. Let's go!"

The sirens scream at us—Run! Run!—
to the brick shelter
marked with a big, black S.

We scramble inside and huddle
with nearly fifty other people,
some in coats, some in pajamas.

I hoist Margaret up on one
of the wooden bunk beds,
stacked four high.
It's damp and dark inside,
lit only by a candle
stuck in a flowerpot,
casting eerie shadows on the wall.

I hold my nose
fighting the smells
of sweat, vomit, urine, and fear.

"We should bring an oil stove inside
to help us stay warm," says one neighbor.

"Don't be daft!" says another.
"It would use up the oxygen!"

Some shelter this is.
Spooky, stinking, suffocating.

## Sounds of Hate

My family and I hunker down,
listen to the
drone of the planes,
the **ack ack ack**
of the antiaircraft guns,
then the high-pitched whistle

and
**BAM!**
of the bombs.

My stomach
drops
with
each
one.

Then there's silence,
ghostly and still.

What has happened?

What's to come?

The A..L..L......C..L..E..A..R sounds—
one long steady note.
We breathe out
a collective sigh,
and get ready to go home . . .

till the sirens wail again.

# MONDAY, 9 SEPTEMBER

## Packing

One more day.
I'm allowed
1 small suitcase (26" x 18")
1 small duffel bag
and my gas mask, of course.
I need my ID card,
my ration card,
2 pairs of pajamas,
2 pairs of pants,
2 pairs of trousers,
2 shirts,
1 pair of shoes,
a hat,
my new warm overcoat
and not much more.

None of my books are permitted,
just a Bible.

I'd rather have my *Dandy* comic books.
Or my Plane Spotter's Guide.

Never mind.
I'm starting my own story now.

## You Can Always Tell a German Plane

Planes are my hobby—
Sunderlands, Spitfires, Hurricanes,
Blenheims, Messerschmitts, Junkers.
I know their names,
I memorized their shapes.
I pester my teachers
and parents with questions.
They shush me,
saying, "So many questions!
Such a chatterbox!"
But I need answers,
so I've pored over books at the library,
ever since England declared war on Germany
a year ago.

I've heard English planes roaring
over the countryside,
doing drills since last year.

Now, the third night of bombing,
I notice German planes
make a different sound from ours.
German planes are diesel.
They throb.

Ours hum.

You never know
when the Germans plan to attack,
but you can tell
by the sound
                    they're here.


## Another Sleepless Night

My head pounds
with the sounds of the planes.
I dread another long night
inside the crowded, smelly shelter,
another morning
staggering round the neighborhood,
blinking in the dust
to see what's left,
who's alive,
                    hurt,
                              missing.

I don't know much about Canada,
but I know this.
They're at peace.
There are no bombs,
no Germans,
no war in this New World.

I'm desperate to get away,
to make the headaches stop.
"Dad, I leave tomorrow, right?"
feeling guilty even as I ask.
How will my family survive
night
after night
after night of this?

"Yes, Ken," says Dad, "tomorrow."

## I'm Off

My dad is at work
(he got a new job
as a postman
and can't risk losing it),
so my stepmum
will see me to
London's Euston train station.

I hug Margaret good-bye
before we leave,
but she doesn't understand
that I'm going,
maybe for good.
" 'Bye, Kenny," she says,
pushing me away
to go play at the neighbor's.

I take one last look around.
Good-bye, house.
Good-bye, home.

## At the Station

Mum and I arrive on the train platform
under the clock,
where crowds of families
mill about,
all waiting,
all watching for the same train.

No crowd of well-wishers for me.

Some dads squat down
to comfort crying kids.
Others hoist sons
high on their shoulders.
No playful punches, funny faces,
or jokes to jolly me along.

"Kenny, stop biting your nails," Mum scolds.
"Stand up straight. Act like a man."

I smile as a tiny girl scolds
her blubbering sister.
"Stop that immediately!
Be British!"
Mums squeeze their eyes shut
as they hold their little ones close,
whisper in their ears.
Loving fingers trace
silky heads, pudgy cheeks.

I wish I had a mum
who would miss me.

I look up at my stepmum.
                    She looks at the clock.


## Wave Me Good-bye

With a screech of brakes,
our train arrives around 11:00 am.

"Well, 'bye, Mum," I say.
"Behave yourself, Ken," she says.
"Don't worry. When the war's over,
you'll make your way home."

There are no tears
from my stepmum,
no clinging,
no hugs,
no lingering last looks.

"I've got to get back now," she says.
"Be good and make us proud.
And whatever you do, don't lose that coat!"

She waves me good-bye,
and that's it.
I raise a hand to wave,

but stop
when I see
she isn't looking.

" 'Bye, Mum," I whisper,
as she hurries away.


## A Shout

Our escorts
check us in
as we board the train.
When I step into the carriage,
I hear my name.
"Ken!
Ken Sparks!"
I glance up
and see a friend.
"Terry? TERRY!"

It's Terry Holmes,
my best neighborhood friend
and football chum
from just up the road.
He's only ten,
but he's a good lad
and a talented artist.
I've always wished
I could draw like him.

"Terry! You're going, too?"

"I couldn't tell you," he says.
"You know—we had to keep it a secret.
I begged to go, though.
I don't know anything
about Canada, but Ken!
We get to sail on a ship
on the Atlantic Ocean."

Terry's excitement lifts my spirits.
"*Oi,* this will be an adventure, all right," I say.
"Did you bring your sketch pad?"
Terry loves to draw ships
more than anything.

"I did. Don't tell!
I sneaked it in my suitcase."

I laugh and give him a shove.
He shoves me back.
The engines gasp and rumble
and in a cloud of steam
and a scream of whistles
we're off.

# Good-bye, London!

I lean my forehead against the window
and watch the houses rush by
to the beat of the wheels rolling the rails.
City melts into suburb,
suburb into country.

I'm leaving
everything behind.

Memories
slide through my head—
my house,
my school,
the girl with braids
who just started to smile at me,
my bike,
my go-cart,
my apple tree.
       I'll miss Margaret.
       I'll miss my dad.

But I'll see them again
when the war is over.

But what if . . .
never mind.
I can't think of what-ifs now.

Good riddance to air raids,
sirens,
nights under the table,
in shelters,
in the Underground.
Good-bye to bombs!

Good riddance to being yelled at.

Terry and I
are on our way,
leaving today,
for a new life
in the New World.
     Good-bye!


## We Are Wrong About the Bombs

I settle back in my seat
and close my eyes . . .
*SCREEEEEEECH!*
What's happening?
Why are we stopping?

"Outside, children!"
yell the escorts.
"Leave your things. Run!"

Terry and I scramble outside.

Wailing sirens fill the air.
"Now they're not even waiting till nighttime!"
I shout.

I run faster,
but trip and
scrape my knee.
Terry pulls me up
and hauls me inside the shelter.
"Thanks, Terry," I say.

We huddle together,
hearts pounding,
cold sweat
drip-
drip-
dripping
down
our
backs.

Minutes go by,
a half hour,
an hour.
Finally
the all-clear sounds.

We climb wearily
back aboard the train
and lurch along—

starting,
stopping,
running,
hiding,
starting,
over and over again.

The train snakes along.
I feel like a thief,
stealing away,
making off with my life.

We've been tracked, hunted down,
our cover about to be blown.

We slink along, mile upon mile,
to a secret port
who knows where. . . .

## The Orphanage

I'm sound asleep
when the train pulls in.
"Ken, Ken," whispers Terry.
"Wake up. We're here."
I open my eyes to see
black tree branches
reaching gnarled fingers up
to the staring moon.

"Where are we?" I ask an escort
as I climb down onto the platform.
"Liverpool," he says.
"On the Mersey, near the coast.
Just a little farther now."

A short bus ride later we enter
a great spiked gate.
What did that sign say?
They're taking us . . . where?
To an orphanage?

Gaping,
we're led off the bus.
"All right, children, line up,"
instructs a woman escort.
"My name is Miss Day," she says,
and then introduces us to the
nine other adults who will be
escorting us on our trip.

One places a hand
on my shoulder,
"No need to chew
your nails, lad.
It will be all right."

I'm not scared.
It's just a bad habit.

We're led
to two grim brick buildings
with long black windows
straight out of Dickens—
boys in one,
girls in the other.

Our escorts shepherd us into a
long school assembly hall.
"Come, lads," says a lanky priest.
"My name is Father O'Sullivan.
We're going to check you in."

We all wear identity discs
on a string round our necks.
As I slip mine out of my shirt,
I can't help feeling sorry
for the small boy blubbering
in front of me.
"John?" says Father O'Sullivan,
reading his tag. "John Snoad, what's wrong?"
John collapses in tears
and another escort picks him up
and takes him out of line.

"Poor little chap. All tired out,"
says Father. "All right, next.
Kenneth Sparks," he reads.
"You're all right, aren't you, boy?"
"Yes, sir."

"Grand. Now see those white mats
down there? Pick one and stuff it with straw."
"What is it for, sir?" I ask.
"It's your bed, darling boy.
Here's a blanket.
Use your pack for a pillow.
Next boy in line."

I look back to see dozens
of boys, tiny and tall,
yawning, scowling, weeping.

I walk over to the mats
and squat down to stuff one.
"We're like seeds in a pod,"
the boy next to me mutters.

A rat scutters across the floor.
I'm not so sure
about leaving home. . . .


## Crying in the Night

I wake to weeping.
It's John Snoad,
on the mat beside me.
"What's wrong?" I whisper.
"I . . . want . . . to . . . go . . . home," says John,
hiccupping between sobs.

"But John, we're on an adventure!
Just think. We'll be real sailors on a ship
with the Royal Navy!"
I pat his arm, try to tell him a bedtime story,
but John only weeps louder.

"Shhh!" say the others. "Pipe down!"
"What's wrong with him?"
whispers Terry on my other side.
"He misses his mum," I say.

Not me.

## Making Friends

In the morning,
Terry and I venture outside
to join the boys racing round
the orphanage schoolyard.

One bloke with wavy brown hair whips by,
trying to catch a little blond lad
who looks just like him.

The little one runs up and hides
behind me, hugging my knees.

"Hey, mate," I say.
"Is that your brother you're hiding from?"
He giggles and crawls through my legs.

"Alan, come here, you worm,"
says the other boy.

"Derek, you can't catch me!" he calls.

"But I can!" I say, scooping Alan up
and flipping him upside down.

"Help! Help!" giggles Alan.

"Thanks, ah . . . ," says Derek.

"Ken. And this is my friend
from home, Terry.
How old is this little chap?"

"Five," says Derek.
"I'm twelve, so Mum said
I have to be the grown-up
and look after him."

"Maw said th' same to me," says a boy
with a thick Scottish brogue
and a younger brother in tow.
"I'm Billy Short,
Peter's five too.
I kin barely keep ahold o'him."

Derek and I exchange glances.
"How old are you, Billy?" asks Derek.
"Nine," he says.

"Nine? Well, old man, we'll help you out," I say,
thinking we'll have to look after Billy, too.

Alan starts to tickle Peter
and they roll in the grass
like puppies.
They make me grin.
"You chaps are lucky," I say.
"I always wanted a brother."

"Careful what you wish for!"
says Derek. "*Oi!* There they go again!"

"Peter, come back!" yells Billy.


## Shrapnel

"*Oi*, look at this, Alan," says Derek,
grabbing his brother by the hand.
"Shrapnel!"
We stop and scoop up
the gray metal bits—
pieces of exploded bombs
and guns—
to add to our collections.
"I found some back home," I say.
"Traded the biggest pieces
for marbles."

No marbles here.
It's just something we do—
pick up the pieces of this war,

wrap our hands round the danger,
try to contain it.

Derek finds the largest lump
and hands it to Alan.
"It's for luck," says Derek.
"For luck!" crows Alan.


## The Shy Kid

A skinny, fair-haired boy
with curls
slumps against a wall, watching us.
I ask Terry, "Who's that?"

"I think his name is Paul," says Terry.
"He doesn't talk much."

I shout, "Hey Paul,
come help us!"

He looks startled,
but then he takes his hands
out of his pockets
and walks over slowly.

"What are you doing?" he asks.

"Collecting shrapnel," I say.

"It's pieces of the bombs!" says Alan.
"Want some?"

"You're playing with bombs?"

"Sure," I say. "They're smashing good fun."
The other boys laugh,
but Paul just stares.

"They can't hurt you now!" says Terry.
"Here's one."

Paul takes the twisted piece of metal,
but when he turns it over
a small ragged edge
cuts his thumb.
"*Ow!*"
It falls
and a small red drop oozes
by his fingernail.

"No thanks," he says,
as he stuffs his finger in his mouth
and walks away.

"Paul, wait!" I shout after him.
But he doesn't turn round.

## Runaways

"Alan, let's . . . ," says Derek.
But Alan is nowhere to be seen.
We were so distracted by Paul
and the shrapnel,
we didn't notice
that the little boys slipped away.
Again!
"They're round here somewhere,"
I say. "I'll help you look."

"Alan! Peter!" we call,
jogging across the schoolyard.
"Maybe they're hiding. Look behind the wall."

No one there, except Paul,
slumped on the ground, nursing his cut.
"Paul, please help us," I say.
"Their brothers are missing."

Paul jumps up and follows.

"Have you seen two little scamps? About five years old?"
I ask a group of girls playing hopscotch.
"No, sorry."

"Wha' will I tell me maw
if I cannae find Peter?" says Billy.

"They're probably just playing
hide-and-seek with us," says Derek.
"Alan! The game is up.
Come on out!"

"Maybe they went inside."
We push open the orphanage door
and peek in the classrooms.
No one.

"Could they have gone across the lawn?" asks Paul.

We gaze across the grass
leading to the open gate
we entered last night on the bus.
Cars speed down the road.
I wince to think of five-year-olds
crossing it.

"We should tell the escorts,"
says Paul.

"But Maw trusted *me* to take care o' Peter,"
says Billy.
And with that, he's off toward the gate.
"Billy, wait!" shouts Derek.
Paul and I have no choice but to follow.

## Sanctuary

Paul stops short.

"I heard laughing,"
he says, turning round and
gesturing to a large willow tree.

Pushing aside the leafy branches
spilling to the ground,
we peer inside.
Peter and Alan are sitting
on either side of one of the lady escorts.
They lean on her shoulders,
smiling up at her with adoring eyes.
She's telling them a story.

"Hello, lads!" says the lady.
"Want to join us?"

"Derek! Billy!" I shout, motioning them over.
"We found them!"

We all creep under the covers
of the branches,
and listen to the story.
It's cozy inside.
I close my eyes
as the words run together
and ripple over each other.

I fall down,
      down,
            down
                  into the story.
I feel safe
for the first time
in a very long time. . . .

## Rude Awakening

"Ken, wake up!" says Terry,
shaking my shoulder.
"You've been asleep forever!"
I sit up, still groggy,
yawning.
"Where are the others?"

"They've just gone in for tea."

Time to eat, yes,
then I can go back to sleep.
Too much excitement,
too many strangers,
too much unknown
trigger a surprising feeling.
I realize I'm longing for home—
with all its warts—
longing for my own bed.

Sirens cut the evening calm.

Escorts shout,
"Run, children, run,"
as they spill out of the classrooms.
"Get your gas masks!"
"Take cover!"

Terry and I tumble
inside the shelter
with the others.

I ask the escorts,
"When are we leaving?
When do we get on the boat?"

"Soon, son, soon."

Another sleepless night jammed together—
elbow to elbow,
knee to knee.

There's no letup,
no escape from the bombs,
no matter how we try
to get away.

Bombs in the city,
bombs on the coast.
Is nowhere safe?

Little John Snoad cries and cries.

# THURSDAY, 12 SEPTEMBER

## Inspections

Morning dawns
with medical inspections.
"Line up, children,"
says Father O'Sullivan.
The doctor looks in my eyes,
my ears, my throat.
He listens to my heart
and checks for
sniffles, coughs, or rashes.
"No diseases must be allowed
to infiltrate the Dominion!"
says Father with a smile.
Terry whispers to me,
"I heard them say
 if you don't pass,
you get sent home."

No way.
I'm not going back!
I'd just be a disappointment
to my parents
                    . . . again.

I laugh and run about
so there's no doubt
I'm ready for anything.

I pass their tests.
So do Terry and my other friends.

Little John Snoad hasn't slept at all
and now he has a bad cold.
But for the first time in days
he isn't crying.
He's all smiles.
"What's he so happy about?" I ask Terry.

"He got his wish," says Terry.
He's going home."

## SS City of Benares

For the rest of us, it's time!
We board a bus
and down to the docks we go,
singing all the way.

The bus rounds a corner and . . .
"Blimey! Terry, look at that!" I say.
"Is that our ship?"
It's the most beautiful thing

I've ever seen—
this mighty ocean liner
called the *City of Benares*—
longer than a football field,
splendid in the sun.
She's not a destroyer,
but a luxury cruise ship
camouflaged in a new coat of gray paint.
She looks stately, regal,
far too important
for poor blokes like us.
"Is she the one?" I ask in disbelief.
"Is she waiting for *us*?"

"Yes, boy, that's our ship,"
says Father O'Sullivan.
"She's the pride of the Ellerman line,
a British steamship
fresh from India.
And we will be joining her
on her first voyage
across the Atlantic."

"Blimey, Terry, look!" I say.
"The size of it!"
The biggest things we'd seen
till then were the old paddle steamers
in the Thames.

We all tumble out of the bus.

Derek and his brother Alan stop short.
*"Cor!"* says Derek. "She's huge!"

"Out of this world!"
says a gap-toothed kid named Fred.
"And if it weren't for this,
we'd never see anything like it."

"Gather round, boys!" calls Father O'Sullivan.
We're going to board soon."

Billy, his little brother Peter,
and Paul get in line behind us.
"How's your finger, Paul?" I ask.
"Better," he says, surprised I remember.
"Ready to go?"
"Ready!"

But for a moment
we stand there
at Princes Landing Stage
just staring,
breathing in the smells
of soot, salt, seaweed, and steam,
the smells of the docks,
of adventure to come. . . .

"Let's go, boys," says Father O'Sullivan.
With a whoop
we scoop up the five-year-olds

and I lead the way,
running
down the docks,
up the gangway
to our ship—
our new home,
our ticket across the sea.

## Welcome, Young Sir!

We boys and girls are met on deck
by a gracious crew—
most of them
sailors from the East.

I've seen men from India
round London, of course,
but never men like these—
sailors decked out in
black shiny shoes turned up at the toes,
and white flowing uniforms,
trimmed with a turquoise sash
and topped with a turban.

"We're in good hands, children,"
says Father O'Sullivan.
"Lascars are some of the best sailors in the world."

We gather in a circle round them,

some kids smiling,
some hiding behind a friend,
some nervously shifting from foot to foot.

The one in charge,
a self-assured young man,
greets us each in turn
with a friendly smile,
"Welcome, young miss,
welcome, young sir.
My name is Ramjam Buxoo.
Welcome to our ship."

Young sir?
People have called me
a lot of things before,
but *no one* has ever called me "sir."
He makes me feel
like an honored guest—
ME—a poor bloke from Wembly.

I step up and say,
"Thank you, sir!"

Mr. Buxoo smiles. "This way, please."
He gestures to the stairs
and then leads the way
to our cabins
in the aft of the ship,
down,

down,
 down,
  to the fourth deck—
  46 boys to port
   44 girls to starboard.


## Cabin Mates

"Fred Steels and Paul Shearing
in here," says Buxoo,
pointing to the first cabin.

"Derek and Alan Capel,
you're in this next one."

"Billy and Peter Short
and Terrence Holmes,
you're down the hall."

"The rest of you boys, this way please."

I look back and wish
I could be with my friends.

"You four in here," says Buxoo,
pointing to me
and three younger boys
I haven't yet met.
They gaze up at me.

One hangs on my sleeve.
One has been crying
and wipes his nose with
the back of his hand.
Another looks bewildered.
I see why they put me
in charge of these lads—
they need someone older
to take care of them.

"Look at this, boys!" I say,
trying to distract them.
"Jolly good!
"We each get our own bunk bed!"

We gape at the beds
laid with geometric quilts,
the large double-door wardrobe,
shiny white porcelain washbasins,
the oversized mirror,
the sturdy chair and desk,
the striped rugs on the floor,
the carafe of fresh water
and the vase of sunny flowers—
everything much finer
than my things at home.
Best of all
we have a porthole
with a view of the sea,
a window to what's ahead.

No more mats on the floor.
No more rats.

Compared to the orphanage,
and even my room at home,
these accommodations
are first rate!
We have our own cabin
on a great fancy SHIP.
*Oi*, it's grand!

I'm going to like it here.


## Time for a Tour

We troop in a group
to the children's playroom,
gawking at the baskets of new toys.

"Where did they come from?" I ask.
"They're donations from people
who wish you well
and want to give you a big sendoff,"
says Buxoo.

I've never had new toys—
couldn't afford 'em.
Things I played with came from
the allotment field

up the street.
If you didn't make your own toys,
you didn't get any.

Here on the *Benares*,
there are shiny new trucks and trains.
Not one has a dent, scrape, or missing wheel.
There's even a child-sized convertible
big enough to climb inside.
Its spick-and-span chrome and paint
puts my go-cart to shame.

The little children gape at
the teddy bears and baby dolls
taking tea with china cups
on a lace tablecloth.

It's a carnival world
here in this playroom,
full of fancy silliness
we've never known.
A fuzzy elephant rides a scooter.
A doll perches atop a pull-toy puppy
while a toy Beefeater stands guard.
Life-size paintings of jesters
and ballerinas dance round the walls.

"*Ooo!* Look at this!"
Some of the littles
reach out to touch

the enormous, finely carved
red rocking horse.

"It's big enough for three of us!"

What catches my eye
are the model airplanes—
mini replicas of the RAF planes
I've seen fly over my house.
I reach for one, but Buxoo stops me.
"No time now.
You must have lunch."
Paul has to pull me away.

We continue down the halls,
peering in posh shops,
dazzling with spotlights, mirrors,
chandeliers, and candelabras,
golden statues and gilded signs
that showcase furs, satins, silks.

Paying passengers
who boarded before us
get a snip and a shave
at the shipboard barber shop
or sway to the music of the orchestra
playing on the Verandah Café.

We pass the bustling galley
with aromas I remember

from the time
before rations.

We enter the grand dining room
with its paneled walls, vaulted ceilings,
and tall vases of fresh flowers.

Altogether it's smashing!
My family certainly never had money
for a holiday like this!

From what I've seen so far,
this ship is like a first-class hotel,
luxury I've never known.
"It's a floating palace
is what it is!" I exclaim.

## Lunch

"This way," says Buxoo.
"There is a special early seating
just for you
before the paying passengers eat."

I sit down on a soft brocade chair
and stare at the menu card
and three different kinds
of knives and forks.
I'm a little confused about

what goes with what.
But no matter.
The menu says
there's chicken for lunch.

"Chicken!" says Derek.
"For as long as I can remember,
we only get chicken
for Christmas!"

Stewards in white turbans,
blue uniforms,
white gloves,
and napkins over their arms
fuss over us.
They pour our water,
asking what we'd like to eat.

"I'd like CHICKEN!" says Derek.
Then he realizes he's shouting
and looks down, embarrassed.
Quietly, he adds,
"Please. Sir."

"May I have, um, um, bangers?"
asks Fred. "Bangers and mash?"

"Fish and chips is my favorite," I say.
"Do you have that? Please?"

"Of course, young sir. Right away."

As the plates come out of the kitchen,
I see food I haven't seen
for months—years—
multiple courses of
filet of beef,
lobster,
shrimp.

And there's fancy food
I've never known.
"Please, sir," I ask a steward.
"What is that?"
"Caviar."
"And that?" asks Derek.
"Foie gras."
"And that?" asks Fred.
"Curry."

It's all delivered
on silver platters
lined with lace doilies.

No roly-poly here!
In fact, nothing here
reminds me of food at home
where I have to work
for every mouthful—
hoeing and weeding vegetables

in our Victory Garden,
checking the chickens for eggs,
and skinning and gutting rabbits for stew.

Here you just ask and the food arrives.
Whatever you fancy!
It's as though Father Christmas
has set up shop
in the kitchen.

I clean my plate.
Derek really tucks in,
sopping up every drop of sauce
with his bread.
We look at each other.
I can tell we're both wondering
if we dare ask for seconds.

We may never get this chance again.
I ask, "Please, may I have some more?"

"Of course you may!"

We eat seconds.
Paul asks for thirds!

Then there's dessert!
Eight courses
are capped with
peaches,

melon,
pineapple—
fruits we haven't seen
for months and months.

There's peach melba
with a star of clotted cream
piped on top.

And OH! ICE CREAM!
Ice cream of every
flavor and color—
rainbow hues of
strawberry,
apricot,
chocolate,
coffee,
peach,
coconut
pistachio. . . .

After the wartime food,
there aren't words to describe it.
We've never eaten so much in our lives.

## Alarm Bells

Just when I lean back,
feeling fat and happy,
alarm bells go off.
I jump up
knocking my plate to the floor.
Paul sputters
and Fred claps him on the back
to keep him from choking.
Billy grips my arm
and everyone stops to listen,
on edge, on alert.
"What now? What's wrong?"
"Are they bombing us again?"

"Keep calm.
Nothing to worry about, children,"
says an officer who strides into the room
as the alarm bells stop.
"I am Chief Officer Hetherington.
Lunch is over and it is time for lifeboat drills.
Come along now. Follow me."

It's officer's orders,
so we all stand and fall in line,
but not before
Paul swallows a last spoonful of ice cream
and Fred crams a roll in his pocket for later.

Hetherington leads us
to our muster station—
the children's playroom.
"If you hear that alarm bell,
you will meet here," he says,
"and await an officer's orders.
We will practice everything
so you will know what to do."

I move a little closer
to Hetherington to hear better.

He hands each of us
a navy blue kapok
waistcoat life jacket.

I put mine on
and tighten the straps.
It's so bulky
I can barely move.

"How does it go?" asks Terry.
"Here, like this," I say.

"You're to wear these
at all times," Hetherington says,
"even in bed,
over your clothes."

"No pajamas?"

asks one little chap.

"No pajamas."
I don't mind sleeping in my clothes,
but how are we going to sleep
in these things?

Next, Hetherington hands us each
a smaller white canvas life jacket.
"Carry this with you
at all times.
When you go to bed,
hang it on
the end of your bunk
beside your shoes and coats."

"Two life jackets?" I ask, incredulous.

But Hetherington isn't looking for debate.
"Yes, young man. TWO!"

## To the Lifeboats

"Now, everyone on deck!"

Once there,
Officer Hetherington assigns
each of us
to a lifeboat.

I get Lifeboat 8.
Hetherington has one boat
lowered down and climbs inside.
"Here, you boy," he says,
pointing to me. "Climb aboard.
Show the others how."

I'm happy he chose me.

Hetherington reaches down
and opens the metal lockers.
"You'll see each boat has
provisions stowed aboard.
Over here is the Fleming gear."

"The what?" I ask.

"The Fleming gear,"
says a girl I don't know.
"You grab that handle
and push and pull it
back and forth
to row the boat."

"How do you know?"

"I was on the *Volendam*," she says.

"The *Volendam*!
The ship that was torpedoed?"

"Whoa!"
  "What?"
    "Torpedoed?"
A murmur of astonished voices
circles the deck.

"That was the ship with hundreds
of children onboard," says Terry.

"Three-hundred and twenty-one," says the girl,
"including me."
"And me!" says a boy standing next to her.
"It's okay, the Royal Navy saved us all."

"But my house had been bombed," the boy
continues. "My family was living in a shelter."

"Mine too," says the girl. "So me and Michael
were squeezed onto this next trip."

"The Navy saved you?"
asks little Alan, eyes wide.
"What's your name?" asks Derek.

"Patricia. Patricia Allen.
And yes, they saved us
because we did lifeboat drills
and we knew what to do."

"Right! Thank you, Patricia and Michael,"

says Hetherington. "Glad to have you aboard.
Now let's get back to our drill."
"Sir?" I ask. "Sir, what if we get torpedoed?"

"Not likely, young man," says Hetherington.
"We're to sail in a convoy of eighteen ships
escorted by a destroyer and two corvettes.
Don't worry. Just make sure
you pay attention
to our lifeboat drills."

I listen hard so,
like Patricia and Michael,
I'll know what to do.


# Mischief

After our drills,
we have free time
to lark about and run the decks.
Terry and I go exploring,
peeking in secret places
we aren't meant to be.

A heavy hand claps me on the shoulder.
"Caught you!" says a gruff voice.
We turn, knowing we're in trouble.

"Scared you, didn't I?" laughs Fred,

the funny kid we met on the docks
with the missing tooth.
"Yes!" says Terry.
"Whatcha doin'?" says Fred
with a mischievous smile.
"Playing spies?"

"No!" I say, getting an idea.
"Let's be stowaways.
Quick! Before they nab us,
back to the lifeboats
where we can hide!"
We dash down the deck.

Glancing round to make sure
we're not being watched,
we climb the davits
and jump into a lifeboat.

Ducking down, we can hear
the conversations of people
passing by.

"Sweetheart, of course I love you!
But don't kiss me here!
It's not proper!"
"*Oi!*" says Terry, his eyes bugging out.
He laughs and starts to make kissy faces at us.
He's ten, but so immature about girls.

"Shhh!" I say. "We don't want to get caught."

Too late.
We hear a harsh voice say,
"Signalman Mayhew,
those kids are
in a restricted area.
Strictly off limits!
See to it immediately."

"Aye, aye, sir!"

A sailor climbs up and
peers down at us.
We're in for it now.

"At ease, boys,"
says Mayhew, helping us down from the boat.
"Steady, now.
I see you're getting your sea legs."

"I'm from a whole family of sailors, sir!"
says Fred. "Got the sea in my blood!"

"Is that so? I . . ."

But he's interrupted by a senior officer
calling the passengers to assemble on deck.
"Attention!" the officer says.
"Attention, all passengers."

We hurry over to hear
what he has to say.
"We have reports that
the Luftwaffe dropped mines
at the mouth of the Mersey last night.
Our departure will be delayed
until tomorrow."

Groans echo around the deck.
                              Fun's over.


## No Safe Harbor

That night
bombs rain down
round the ship,
now moored
in the middle of the river.
There's nowhere to run,
no place to take cover.
We're more trapped than ever,
like fish in a barrel.

Will we survive this night?

## Bad Luck

A nasty day dawns with wet weather.

Derek, Alan, and I go on deck,
rain splattering our faces.
We crawl under a stairway
and peer out at the black clouds,
ominous with a growl of thunder.
*CRASH!*
"I don't like it!" cries Alan,
covering his ears.
"It's okay, we'll go back inside," says Derek.
"Coming, Ken?"

"No, I'll stay here a bit."
There's no wind.
The flags sag
by their posts.
I stare out at the water—
my way out of this war.
I hope.

A group of sailors stop nearby,
not noticing me
under the stairs.
"We won't sail today," says one.
"It's Friday the 13th!
Every sailor knows that's bad luck."
"No choice, chap," says another.
"Our destroyer has to meet
an incoming convoy
from Canada in five days.
It's carrying war supplies
and the war won't wait."

Bad luck?
They sound worried.
A lone foghorn warns of danger.

Chief Officer Hetherington
comes through the door
and the sailors straighten up and salute.
"Captain Nicoll advises
the mines have been cleared
from the channel," says Hetherington.
"We leave today."

## It's Time

At last, at long last!
I feel like a wind-up toy

whose key has been
twisted and tightened
for too long,
and now they're finally letting go!
It's 6:15 pm on Friday the 13th
when the *City of Benares*
and Convoy OB 213
steam out in the steady rain.

"I think it's a jolly good sign," says Derek.
"Thirteen is my lucky number!"
"Mine, too!" says little Alan.

Despite the darkening skies,
despite the rain turning to sleet,
I'm lit up with relief to get away,
eager for all that's to come.
I close my eyes
and the fresh breeze
blows all my troubles behind me
like the black smoke
billowing back from the stacks.

The ship picks up speed,
slicing a path through the water,
leaving my sorry past in our wake.
I wonder what's ahead. . . .

Terry, by my side,
leans out over the rail
and shouts to the sailors

and dockside workers
waving ashore.
"Good-bye! Good-bye!"
I clap him on the back
and he grins.

Someone starts singing
and we all join in:
*"Wish me luck*
*as you wave me good-bye. . . ."*
Faces beam as the wind picks up,
the port flags
snap to attention,
and the horns bellow farewell.
Liverpool disappears
in a mist of fog
as we leave the war behind
and head west toward the sun.


## Reinforcements

We lean over the rail to watch
our Royal Navy convoy
assemble round us.

I count eighteen ships
sailing in formation—
nine columns, two ships in each,
surging west.

We steam up the center,
taking our place
as the flagship.

In the distance, miles ahead,
I can see our destroyer
and two corvettes
leading the way,
the arrowhead of
our defense—
with a seaplane
keeping watch from above.

"That's a Sunderland,"
I yell to my friends,
pointing up at the plane.
"They call it a flying boat."

"How do you know?" asks Derek.

"Planes were my hobby back home.
I know all of them."

"He does, too," says Terry.
"And I know all the ships."

Terry gets out his sketch pad,
drawing the liners, freighters,
tankers, and smaller boats
that stretch as far as the eye can see.

He draws quickly,
giving the ships line,
shadow,
substance.
I wish I could do that,
make something from nothing.
I look out to the horizon.
What *can* I do?
What's to become of me?
When I look back,
Terry has drawn me—
a boy at the rail,
surrounded by strong ships,
leading the way
to a new life.
This is really happening!

The engines throb
as we make our way
through the dark.


## Our First Night

Down to bed at 8 pm,
but no one can sleep.
My stomach rolls
to the pitch of the sea
and after all that food—*oof!*
I crawl into bed

in the pitch black,
but one of the little boys calls out.
"Ken, will you tuck me in?"
"Me too."
"I miss my mummy," says another.
I stand up to try to comfort them
but the ship tilts
and *wham!*
I slam into the bedpost.
*Oww!*
I hear coughing
as someone gets sick
over the side of the bed.
I gag at the smell.
Turning on the light for a minute,
I try to clean up the mess
as best I can.
"Close your eyes now
and I'll tell you a story," I say.
"Once there was a brave boy
named Wart who met a wizard
named Merlyn. . . ."

We're all in need of a little magic right now.

## Storms

Come morning
I stagger to the porthole
to see if our luck has changed.
High swells and more sleet
batter the boat.
The boys in my cabin
wake up whimpering—
seasick,
homesick.

"I'll go get help,"
I say. "I'll be right back."

I knock on Father O'Sullivan's door.

A weak voice answers, "Come in."
Father's in bed, pale and coughing.
"I'm not feeling well," he says.
"Don't come too close."

"The boys are all seasick and

I don't know what to do."

"Go ask the galley for a
bit of barley sugar water," he says.
"It will help."

I retrieve the sugar water
and head back.
The ship rolls
and I'm thrown
against an officer on deck.

"Whoa, boy!" he says.
"Where are you going?
What's your name?"

"Ken, sir," I say. "Ken Sparks."
"Steady there," he says.
"I'm Fourth Officer Cooper.
Ronnie Cooper.
Let's get you back below.
A German bomber
has been sighted.
Best to take cover."

"Yes, sir. Yes, Officer Cooper."

Even here at sea,
we're not out of the woods.

## Steady as She Goes

Even before I open my eyes
Sunday morning
I feel something has changed.

Heat and light pour into the cabin
through the porthole.
The incessant rolling
has stopped.
"Lads, get up!" I say.
The sun is out!"

At the top of the stairs,
I stop short,
squinting,
as blinding sparkles dimple the sea,
sky and water
reflecting blue on blue.
Fresh salt air
makes me breathe deeply
and as the escorts gather
us for prayers,

the sun warms my face,
like a blessing,
a congratulation.
Calmness and peace
lap like little waves.

## A Different War, A Different Fight

Soon the decks echo
with shouting—
the good kind—
the sounds of kids having fun.

Fred and I walk down the deck,
trying to decide
whether to join the
lassoing contest,
the drawing contest,
the sing-along,
the game of shuffleboard,
or deck tennis.

"There's everything you can
think of for a kid," says Fred.
He's right.

"Hey, that's not fair," I say,
pointing to a tug of war
with big kids on one side

and three little ones on the other.
Fred and I run to the short end,
wrapping our hands round the rope.
"Pull! PULL!"
We lean back with all our might,
but the other side pulls us forward.
Back and forth, back and forth
until. . . . Ah!
Someone slips
and we all topple together, laughing,
a heap on the ground.

Fred and I scoot to the side of the deck
and lay out in the sun,
propping our life jackets
under our heads as pillows.

"Blimey, this is the life," I say.
Must be what it feels like
to live like society,
sunning yourself on a ship on the sea. . . .

I've just closed my eyes
when some other chaps
have a different idea
for those life jackets.
"Pillow fight!" they yell,
thumping us good.
      I jump into the fray,
          feeling like a kid again.

## Smile for the Camera

"Look over here, lads,"
says a slim Scottish lady in a beret
aiming a camera at us
as we swat each other.

She must be one of the paying passengers.
Never seen her before.

"Is that a movie camera?" I ask,
hurrying over to inspect it.

"Yes," she says, "I'm Miss Grierson.
I'm making a film about you
and your friends going to Canada."

Girls pass by, in awe.
"She's wearing trousers!" whispers one.
"And she has the most magnificent
long cigarette holder I've ever seen!"

"Don't mind me. Go on with your games,"
says swanky Miss Grierson, puffing away.

She follows us and I follow her,
asking questions,
always keen to volunteer.
"Have you been to Hollywood?
Can I hold your camera?

Can I try your cigarette?"
The answer is always, "No,"
but she points the camera at me
and I smile.

Just think.
In the New World,
I'll be safe,
    *and* I'll be a movie star.


## A Jolly Holiday

At meals, we stuff ourselves silly.
Some kids have to rush out at times
to hang their heads over the rail,
and as Father O'Sullivan says,
"pay their respects to the sea."
But then they go back in,
a bit green round the gills,
but ready to take on more ballast!

Derek says,
"Aboard the *Benares*,
it's a Christmas dinner every meal."

All in all,
          it's a jolly good holiday.

## Progress

Wave,
        after wave,
            mile
                after mile
                    we sail farther
                    and farther
                        from where the planes
                            and the U-boats prowl.


Wave
        after wave
                        I wonder
                            "Are we safe yet?"


Wave
        after wave
            I ask officers,
                "Spotted any more German bombers?"


Finally, I hear an officer's answer that makes me smile.
"Here, on this route, the first two days
may contain an element of danger,
but afterwards we should be quite all right."

# MONDAY, 16 SEPTEMBER

## Day Three

After our daily lifeboat drills,
I look at the sun
and notice
we're zigzagging.

"Smart boy," says a cadet.
"What's your name?"
"Ken, sir."
"Mine's Critchley. Doug Critchley.
We zig
           and zag
to throw the enemy off course.
No easy feat
for a convoy three miles across!

But we're almost clear, Ken.
Once we're five hundred miles out,
we'll be safe."

## Secret Stowaways

While the doctors aren't looking,
sickness sneaks aboard.
It starts with Alan.
"What's that rash on your arm?" asks Derek.
"It's ouchy!" says Alan.
"Don't scratch it!" I say.

Too late.
One bump turns to two,
to twelve,
to twenty.
"Peter, don't touch Alan!" I say.
Too late.
They both break out in spots—
chicken pox!

"It's off to the infirmary for you two,"
says Father O'Sullivan
who coughs and sneezes—
*ACHOO!*
He's feverish with flu.

But the doctors say, "Don't worry.
"Everyone will be all right.
And soon we'll be in Canada."

Hope is contagious.

## In the Clear?

Day four,
morning rain,
cold and wet.
Once again my insides
pitch and plunge
in time with the waves,
but I'm lucky,
I don't throw up
like the other kids.
Gale winds are starting to build.
The escorts say to stay below.

The day passes quietly,
reading, napping,
and playing cards,
but by dinner,
I go on deck to see
all the colors of a rainbow
arching over our heads.

Smiles and cheers

say by now
we *must* be in the clear.

"Are we, Officer Cooper?" I ask.
"Are we safe?"
"We're six hundred miles out," he says.
"Should be smooth sailing from now on."

## Huzzah!

Relief washes over us all,
kids and grown-ups alike,
like a rain shower
rinsing off the built-up grime
of worry and fear.

How we feast and celebrate,
eating extra ice cream tonight!
At eight o'clock, we head down to bed
turning thoughts
to our new homes
all over Canada
and our shiny new lives ahead.

## Safe at Last

"We're okay now,
aren't we, Ken?"

ask the little boys
who share my cabin.
"Can we take our life jackets off?
Can we put on our pajamas?"

"Yes! Didn't the escorts tell you
today in the playroom?
They told us we could.
Hang up your vests.
Take off your life jackets.
We're safe now.
We're six hundred miles from England,
six hundred miles from war.
U-boats don't come out this far."

Like hermit crabs
shedding their shells,
we strip off our bulky life jackets
and pull on clean, soft pajamas.
I turn out the lights and say,
"Good night, lads.
Sleep tight.
Soon we'll be in Canada. . . ."

I drift into dreams,
                    safe at last
                            safe at last. . . .

## *BAM!*

I jolt awake,
jumping up in the dark.
The floor shudders,
              the night split with sounds of
                              splintering wood,
              creaking metal,
                              clattering glass.
Then . . .
                  nothing.

The world stands still,
silent and dark.

                              Was it a bad dream?

Seconds later,
panicked footsteps
outside in the hall,
rushing water.
              Bells sound the alarm—
                      *Emergency! Emergency!*

Tearful gasps from my cabin mates,
        "Ken? KEN! What is it? What's wrong?"

I'm wet.
        Am I bleeding?

I smell smoke,
sulfur,
           explosives,
                    burning wood.

Bile rising,
           I swallow it down.
                    WHAT'S HAPPENING?

Then I know—
           we've been hit!
                    *Torpedoed.*

I can't see anything,
so I feel my way in the dark,
damaged door
           shattered wall.
Blue bulbs cast a ghostly path down the hall.

I tell myself it will be all right.

I say aloud, "Boys, it's okay."
No fear.
We trained for this
every day, twice a day.

"Off we go, then!" I say,
keeping my voice chipper.
"Stiff upper lip, boys."
Life jackets.

Calm, quiet,
walk, don't run
to the muster station.
Hurried steps echo
down the halls.
We trained for this.
We know what to do.

## Cadet Critchley

"Boys, do not wait.
Go to your lifeboats.
You trained for this.
You know what to do."

"Yes, sir!"

*WAIT!*
My coat!
I forgot my coat,
the overcoat my stepmum bought me.
"Ken, you must keep an eye on it!" she said.
Blimey, if I go home without that coat,
Mum will kill me.

I nip back to get it.

I have to push my way
against the surge of children
scrambling to the stairs

and wade through floating debris.
Water's rising
as I step over
busted doors,
splintered furniture,
and a mass of broken glass
littering the halls.
Where is my cabin?

There!
I push open the door
to find the
room flooding,
water spewing
from broken pipes.
Cold, wet,
I wrap my warm wool coat around me,
remembering my family
back home
in trouble too,
     braving the *Blitz*,
     braving the bombs.


## To the Lifeboats!

I struggle back down the hall,
up the main staircase,
through the dining rooms,
and onto the deck.

The hatches have been blown off,
the emergency lights are on.
Electrical sparks shoot up
from the ironwork.

The noise hurts my head—
steam, sirens, wind, rain.
"Watch it there, boy!" shouts an officer,
grabbing my arm.
I step carefully around a gigantic hole.

Where's my lifeboat?
Lifeboat 8.

Am I late?
        Too late?

I trained for this.
I knew what to do.
I look fore and aft.
Going fast,
I crash into others
wild-eyed, open-mouthed,
racing the other way.
I catch sight of an escort
carrying a girl covered in blood,
hear shouting,
whimpering,
calling,
bawling.

There!
It was that way!
I dash down the decks,
wind whipping my hair,
rain stinging my face.


          My lifeboat is gone.


## Lost

I rush down
the starboard deck,
but all the lifeboats
have been launched.
I run over to port.
The winds howl,
I hear children crying.
Is anyone left
          to save me?


## Lifeboat 12

"Here, boy!
Here's one with room,"
says Officer Cooper,
stationed at Lifeboat 12,
the rear boat on the port side.

Cooper picks me up
and tosses me down
to someone else I recognize—
Ramjam Buxoo,
the young Lascar
who greeted us
when we first boarded the ship.

"Ken!"
I turn and see my friends
Paul, Fred, Billy, and Derek at the far end.
There's a new boy nearest me.
"Sit down! Sit by Howard," shouts Derek.

"Derek, Billy, where are your brothers?"
I yell. "Where's Terry?"
But screams drown out
my questions as
the ship starts to roll.
The crewmen on deck
brace themselves and struggle
to hold the ropes on pulleys
that keep the lifeboat level.

A lady on deck—
the escort
who told us stories under the tree—
wants to wait,
won't let us leave.

"My girls!" she cries,
"I don't see the girls in my care!"

"Mary! Mary Cornish!"
calls another escort. "They're safe.
They're in another boat
with Mrs. Towns."

"Prepare to abandon ship!"
yells Cooper.
And still Miss Cornish hesitates.
The ship lurches farther to port.

*Lady, c'mon!* I think. *We've got to go!*

Cooper says, "Miss, Steward Purvis
checked the playroom and the cabins.
No one else is coming, Miss,"
he adds in his gentle Scottish accent.
"It's time to go."

Miss Cornish catches her breath.

Cooper looks in her eyes,
then with a small nod of his head
gestures at me
and my friends.
She nods
and steps aboard.

She settles in the midst of us boys
and tries to reassure us,
discounting the danger.
"It's all right," she says,
rubbing our shoulders.
"It's only a torpedo."

Only!
Is she mad?

## Abandon Ship!

"Steady, men!" yells Cooper.
"She's slipping in the stern
and rolling to port."
The crew
desperately tries
to level the lifeboat
swinging from the davits.

"Clear away the boat,
man the falls and reels," orders Cooper.

"Stand by for lowering.
Lower away!
Handsomely now!"

I see Lifeboat 12 is one of the last to go.

It falls quickly,
my stomach dropping,
everyone screaming,
hands clutching the rails
like monkeys.

## Down to the Sea

D

O

W

N

we drop,
falling,
frantic,
on a fiendish ride
bound
where?
To drown
in a watery grave?
But no,
we don't tip
or flip
like so many lifeboats
seesawing down

the side of the ship,
flinging men,
women,
children,
officers,
crewmen and cooks,
screaming
forty feet down
to the sea,
to the roiling sea.

We hit with a *thud,*
but we don't swamp
or flood
like so many lifeboats we see
with passengers
sitting waist deep in water.

Purvis and four Lascars
who had lowered the boat
from the deck
now scramble down a rope ladder
to join us in the lifeboat.
Last to come is Cooper.
"Pull away from the ship,"
he orders.

But wait!
Four more Lascars
scramble down the ropes.

"Back!" says Cooper. "Pick them up."
They jump into the boat.
"Now lay off, get clear!"


## Rescue Will Come

In the hail and gale,
our boat surfs up
and sleds down the swells,
each wave high as a house.

Water slops in
and the crew bails with buckets,
hands, shoes, and hats.

I tell myself it will be all right.
The Royal Navy will come
as they did for the *Volendam*
where all were saved but one.
Our convoy will be here soon.

The other boys and I
clutch the gunwales,
white-knuckled,
open-mouthed,
and yes,
half enjoying
the thrill ride
of slamming up and down

the waves—
better than
any ride at the fairground.
Paul huddles in the bow
with Miss Cornish,
watching us shout.

Soaked to the bone,
stoked with suspense,
I tell myself this is IT!
This is the story
I'll tell my friends
if I don't die first.
A ship *will* come
to rescue us.

Just hold on, hold on, you've got to hold on.

## Horror

Two more explosions
flash in the night,
the light
exposing a horror show—
people clinging to
overturned lifeboats,
swimming to
overloaded rafts,
grabbing at

floating deck chairs
with flailing arms
beseeching hands.

Voices snatched by the wind—

"Help me please!"
                    "Grab my hand!"

                                    *"Bachao!"*
"I've got you!"
                    "Dear God, have mercy!"

*"Allah!"*
                    "I can't swim!"

"There's a raft. Grab on!"
                    "Lord, help us!"

          "Let go! You're pulling me under!"

    *"Madat kar!"*

"There's no more room! You'll drown us all!"

"It's cold, so cold."

          "Mummy! I want my mum!"

Billy throws up over the side.

"What can we do?" I shout.
"We've got to help them."

But there are so many people in the water,
in the dark,
in distress—
SOS! SOS!
Twenty-foot waves
cresting,
crashing,
smashing.
Rain turning to sleet.
It hurts to look.
People are swimming and sinking,
slamming into boats, rafts,
jetsam and flotsam,
slipping and surfacing,
sliding and
OH!
                    sucked under. . . .


## Up from the Sea

I see something rise in the water,
something ahead.
It's the fine red rocking horse
from the children's playroom.
It rears up from the sea,
the red horse of war,

its mouth open,
silently screaming
at all it sees,
rocking up and down
in the waves
past the bodies of those
I now know
are already
dead.

## Heroes

Our lifeboat is nearly full,
but our captain Cooper steers
through the wild waves,
through the hail,
through the gale,
to the rafts and pulls people aboard.
One's Cadet Critchley.
There's Signalman Mayhew
and six Indian Lascars
I haven't met.

"Peard, over here!"
yells Cooper.
But Peard
refuses a hand up.
Splashing, thrashing
through the water,

we see him
rescue a boy,
pull him to a raft,
hand him up,
then swim off
to rescue another.
He's a hero, he is,
saving all those children.
I want to be just like him.

But then
watching him struggle
through the waves,
I think,
heroes can't die.
                    Can they?


## Get Away!

The *Benares* shudders and groans,
slipping farther down
into the water.
"She's going down!" shouts Cooper.
"Man the Fleming gear!
Get us away
or she'll suck us down with 'er!"

"I can help!" I say. "I know how."
"That's the stuff, young man," says Cooper.

I crawl over people
to sit with the sailors
working the Fleming gear.
Push! Pull!
Push! Pull!
We work the levers
that move the bar,
    that turn the gears,
        that propel our boat
            away
              away
            away from the sinking ship.

## Blues on the Run

We row and row and row.
Far off we hear sounds high on the wind—
voices from another lifeboat.
They're singing!

*"Rule Britannia! rule the waves;*
*Britons never will be slaves. . . ."*

I sing too as I row . . .
    *"Roll out the barrel. . . ."*
Then loudly, defiantly, everyone joins in.
    *"We've got the blues on the run. . . ."*

# Blankets

A safe distance from the ship
we stop rowing.
Steward Purvis
pulls out blankets
from lockers under the floorboards.
"How many are there?" asks Cooper.
"Fifteen," says Purvis.

I look around the boat.
There are nearly fifty of us,
wet and shivering.
Not enough. Not enough.
Most go to the crewmen in cotton tunics
who have no coats,
and we boys will share two.

# Fireworks

Suddenly
all the *Benares'* lights
blaze on,
dazzling in the night.
Some electrical fault
has tripped the switch.
"She looks just like a Christmas tree!"
says Fred.
Reflections,

quicksilver twinkles
dot the water
as hissing red flares
dash upward
to the clearing skies
and the gaping moon.

One ghostly torch moves
round the top deck and bridge
of the ship.

"Look!" says Fred.
"I'll bet that's Captain Nicoll
making one last round."

A huge searchlight
on the horizon
sweeps the seas.
Is it the U-boat
looking to finish us?
I quickly crouch down
and work faster—
pushpullpushpull
getawaygetawaygetaway—
as the moon ducks
behind a cloud.

## Going Down

There's an awful noise
of twisting metal.
"Look! There she goes!" I shout.
"Ohhh!" gasps Miss Cornish,
covering her mouth.
We sit helplessly
about three hundred feet away
watching as the *Benares*—
our getaway ship,
our adventure,
our "floating palace"
with its playroom of toys
and its shops of jewels
and its feasts of chicken and lobster and chocolate
and peaches and melon and pineapple and . . .
oh!. . . ice cream,
and its Captain Nicoll
        up,
            up,
                and upends

            and slick with oil

                slides down the waves

                    with a bang and a groan.

                        Gone.

## Shock

I stare
at the place
where the waves close over the ship.

"We should record the time," says Cooper.
"Who else has a watch?"
"Here," says Father O'Sullivan. "I have 10:34."
"Half an hour," says Cooper, grimacing.
"That's all it took."

It's like the *Benares* went to its own grave.
It's hard to believe that
our big beautiful ship
and our glorious life aboard
ever really existed. . . .

## Yo!

A cry from the water
brings me back to life.
Cooper spots one last man,
the one who refused a hand up.
He's finally spent.
Cooper calls out,
"Gunner Peard! Harry!
Here! Over here!
Take my hand!"

He pulls him aboard.

"Thanks, mate," says Peard.

"Did your lifeboat swamp?" asks Cooper.

"Dunno. Never made it to 'er," says Peard.
"Was at my gunner station
when the torpedo hit
and I went straight inter the drink
on impact.
Been swimmin'
for half an hour now!"

And yet Peard straightens up
and yells, "Chins up!"
From that moment on,
Peard is on the move,
forging his way through the crowd,
foul-mouthed and loud
bossy, unbowed.
Strong and tough,
short and gruff,
he's a salty sea dog
straight from my storybooks.

I gaze up at Cooper
and think about the quiet bravery,
the kindness,
that saved Peard—

the roughneck
who rescued all those children.
One man reserved,
      one raucous.
                Neither much taller than me.
                Heroes both.


## Questions

Where are the eighteen ships
in our convoy?
Where is our destroyer?
Our corvettes?
When are they coming to fetch us?
                      What if they're not?


## I Can't Move

So many arms and so many legs jammed crammed together
no leaning no slouching no room to stretch or twist or turn
or lay back except for

Father O'Sullivan, weak with flu,
sprawling in the bottom of the boat.

Squashed side by side,
elbow to elbow,
knee to knee,

packed together
like our lifeboat rations
of sardines in a can,
we try to sleep.

## A Light in the Night

A torch, then two! Here they are—
At last!
Our rescue.

## Ahoy!

It's not a ship,
it's another lifeboat.
They call to us.
The waves have calmed,
so the boat can pull up alongside.

"The name's Paine,"
says their lifeboat captain.
"We're from the *Marina*,
part of the convoy."

"Where *is* the convoy?"
asks Father O'Sullivan.
"When are they coming
for us?"

Paine glances at Cooper.
Cooper clears his throat.
"Might as well know the truth, Father,"
he says. "No one expected
we would be attacked this far out.
Our destroyer left last night
to help escort another ship."

"But where are all the other ships?"

Paine sighs.
"After a U-boat attack,
naval rules require
all convoy ships
to scatter to avoid further casualties.
The Germans sank the *Marina*, too.
But don't worry.
I'm sure Captain Nicoll
radioed an SOS to high command
and a rescue ship is on its way.
Seen any other lifeboats?
We had two
for our crew."

We have only found each other.
Cooper and Paine agree to stick together
till dawn.

## Keep Calm and Carry On

I try to go to sleep.
We'll be picked up tomorrow
or the day after that.

The Royal Navy will save us
and we'll go home heroes. Right?

A wave hits me in the face.

## Awakening

Winds rising
white caps
cold spray
storm gray.

Morning's light
reveals
a shocking scene—
it's just us
and the *Marina*'s sixteen men
for as far as the eye can see.
Stone cold seas
stretch out north, south, east, and west,
with nothing between us
and the ends of the earth.
Where are the other lifeboats?
How did we get separated?
Did they sink?
Is everyone dead?

I ask Father O'Sullivan.

"I don't know, son," he says.
"Maybe we just drifted faster
because our boat wasn't full of water."

All we know is this—
we and the *Marina*'s lifeboat
are alone
      on a vast and empty sea.


## A Decision

"We've decided to set sail
for Ireland,"
I hear Paine tell Cooper.
"We should make land
in a week."

Would we go, too?

Officer Cooper
looks at us,
at our overloaded boat.
"No, safer to wait
where the *Benares* went down.
Then the rescue ship
can find us."

"God be with you," calls Father O'Sullivan.
"And with you," shouts Paine.

I watch the other lifeboat go,
then turn to my friends.
We look each other in the eyes,
but no one speaks.
We look down,
all wondering the same thing.
Which captain
made the right choice?

## Change Places

Captain's orders:
All British men back to the stern.
All other crewmen amidships.
All passengers forward to the bow.

Ramjam Buxoo
translates the orders
for his men.
Officer Cooper nods
to him in gratitude.

Slow-
ly,
care-
fully,
one
by
one,

we re-
arrange
our-
selves
so as
not
to
tip,
or
flip,
or
flood
the boat.

## Shelter

There is none.
"Hang on," says Steward Purvis
pulling out a canvas tarp.
"We can use this."
He and Signalman Mayhew
fasten it across the bow.
"Now two adults
or three of you boys
can fit underneath
and take turns napping
out of the wind."

Derek pops inside

and sticks his head out.
The businessman
Mr. Nagorski starts to laugh.
"He looks like a duck,
coming out of its hole."
From then on,
we call the tent Duck's Hole,
our tiny hidey-hole,
away from the glaring sun
and the salty spray
that stings our cuts.


## All Aboard

With nothing to do,
I count our crew:
6 boys
5 British sailors
32 Lascars
1 businessman
1 priest
and
1 lady in a lifeboat of men.

Forty-six souls in thirty feet of timber,
shorter than a London bus.

## Supplies

Steward George Purvis
is busy digging under seats
and floorboards,
taking inventory
of the supplies
our lives
depend on.

I crane my neck to see what he finds:

>  1 sail, rudder, tiller
>  1 set of flares
>  2 axes
>  1 bucket
>  1 small first aid kit
>  1 oil lamp with oil
>  1 box waterproof matches
>  1 sea anchor
>  1 can of grease.

"The compass is damaged,"
Purvis reports.
Disastrous news.
How will we find land without a compass?

We'll have to use
the rising and setting sun
to gauge east and west

and look to the stars
to find true north.

I think of my books
about adventure at sea
and only then do I realize what else we're missing:
    a radio
    a sextant
    charts
    flags
    fishing gear
            No way to find our way.
            No way to find more food.


## Provisions

We'll make do with what we've got.
Purvis digs down
into the metal lockers
and reports what he finds:
    ship's biscuits
tins of:
    sardines
    salmon
    corned beef
    pineapple
    peaches
    condensed milk

After our glorious nine courses
and extra ice cream
on the *Benares*,
we're back to this.

                              Rations.


## Water

"How much water?" asks Miss Cornish.
"There are two large canisters," says Purvis,
"about sixteen gallons in all.
Enough if we portion it out."

The sight of the water cans
reminds me
how thirsty
I am
already.

"Can we please have water?" I plead.
"Yes, water!" says Derek.
"Water!" the boys all shout.
"Soon," says Purvis. "Very soon."
                    Not soon enough.

## Forbidden

My throat is scratchy
and my tongue shriveled.
The sounds of salt water
lapping,
swishing,
swirling,
teasing,
torture me.
I dip my hand
in the drink
ready to cup
some precious drops.

"STOP!"
orders the captain.
"DO NOT DRINK THE SEAWATER!"
He explains,
"It will make you thirstier.
It will make you mad.
It will kill you."

I remember a line
from one of my books:
"Water, water, everywhere
Nor any drop to drink."

I gaze out at the ocean,
salty blue water

as far as the eye can see,
and only now
does that line
make sense.


## Calculations


A rescue ship will come.
We know it will.

BUT
if it doesn't
in a day,
the officers say
we will sail for Ireland.
Officer Cooper looks at his watch,
studies the sun,
consults the other officers,
calculates the distance to land.
I feel the wind blowing;
today, it feels like a friend.

The officers are hushed,
but catching my eye,
Cooper smiles at me
and gives a thumbs up.
He's not giving up hope,
so neither will I.

"This southwesterly wind
will keep us moving east,"
Cooper tells us.
Mr. Nagorski works his way
to the stern
to talk with the officers.
He returns to the bow to confirm
we're about six hundred miles from land,
about eight days' sail.

It's far,
but maybe we can make it.
                              If their guess is right.


## Water Rations

What's the least amount of water
we need to survive each day?
I see Steward Purvis count
the people aboard
and do the calculations.

He announces, "We will each be allowed
two small dippers of water a day,
one at noon,
one at night.
That way we'll have
enough for about eight days."

But I wonder,
are we six hundred miles from land?
Is eight days of water enough?

## First Lunch

"Time to eat,"
says Steward Purvis,
taking charge of our first meal—
one hard ship's biscuit the length of my finger,
one slice of corned beef on top,
one dipperful of water.

Each bit of food is passed down
from the stern,
hand by hand,
first to us children,
then to Buxoo's crewmen,
and finally to the British staff
until all forty-six are served.
The process takes forever,
nearly three-quarters of an hour!

Then Purvis dips the thumb-sized metal cup
into the water tank and
sends it down the line.
No one is allowed to sip slowly.
The little cup must be
passed back right away
so others may drink.

When it's my turn,
I see the cup holds just a few mouthfuls.
I tip it to my lips
and pass the cup back.

I hold the water
in my mouth for a moment.
I roll it over
my cheeks and tongue—
a cool bath
that douses the fire
of that devil thirst.

Then the water
slides down my throat
and is gone.

"Please! Just one more drink?"
Paul begs, no longer shy.
"It's nae enough," says Billy.
"Please, Georgy Porgy!" says Derek
with a twinkle in his eye. "Puddin' and pie!"
Georgy Porgy flashes a smile of affection
but is firm with our food rations,
unmoved by
pleas, complaints,
glares, or groans.

I'm still hungry.

Still thirsty.

But it will have to be enough
to last eight days.
In eight days we'll be saved.

If their guess is right.

# If Only . . .

If only I could
move a little,
stretch my stiff legs.
*"Ooch! Jings!"* says Billy,
when I kick his shin by mistake.
"Sorry."
With forty-six people
there are elbows in your back,
knees in your side,
feet in your face.
There's no room to move
from your little space.

I shift in my seat
and think of my bike
back home.
How I loved to ride that bike!
Pedals pumping,
coasting—
it felt like freedom.

Dad got it for me
at the allotment field.
One of the wheels had buckled,
so someone chucked it.
Dad said, "Here, you can mend that."
And I did.

We kids made our own fun
or we didn't have any.

I made my go-cart
out of old pram wheels.
Terry and I would fly down the street
past the rag-and-bone man.

If only Terry were here. . . .
If only I knew where he was,
whether he was safe. . . .
Do my parents know what's happened?
Is anyone thinking of me?

I remember Terry's drawing of me
staring happily out to sea.
Was that really just six days ago?


## Barriers

Different languages
and our seating arrangements

form three islands in the boat:
British staff in the stern,
Lascars in the center,
Father O'Sullivan, Mary Cornish, and Mr. Nagorski
sitting with us children
in the bow.

Two men are bridges
between us—
only Gunner Harry Peard
and Ramjam Buxoo
are nimble enough
to move carefully
about the boat,
knowledgeable enough
to translate
the different
languages aboard.
Buxoo and Peard act as ambassadors,
messengers, negotiators.

"Blast!" explodes Peard.
"Hurry that food along, Purvis.
These poor little blighters are half starved!"

Ambassador yes,
but unlike Buxoo,
Peard is no diplomat.

## Understanding

I notice one of the younger Lascars,
with the start of a mustache I envy,
sitting just on the other side
of Miss Cornish.
He talks and talks to his mates,
but I can't understand
what he's saying.
He notices me, looking at him.
I notice he looks thirsty, tired, and cold.
I smile at him. It means, "Me, too."
He smiles back.
We can't talk to each other,
but we both understand.

## Already Heroes

Up in the bow,
we tell stories to pass the time.
"I was trapped in my cabin
after the torpedo hit,"
says Father O'Sullivan.
"Derek and Billy pulled me out.
You boys are already heroes!"

But Derek and Billy
hardly smile.
All they talk about

are their little brothers.
"Did anyone see Peter?"
asks Billy.
"Or Alan?" asks Derek.
"They were in the infirmary
when the torpedo hit.
We don't know
what happened to them."

"I'm sure they're all right," says Father.

"The nurses probably got them
into another lifeboat," I say.

"We promised our parents
we would look after 'em,"
says Billy, swiping his eye
with the back of his hand.

Everyone says Derek and Billy
are heroes for saving Father O'Sullivan.
But they don't think so.

Heroes don't lose their little brothers.


## Bail, Matey, Bail!

No matter what we do,
we're sitting in water most of the time.

"Bail with your hands, like this," I say.
"Cup 'em and toss the water overboard."

"*Oo*, it's so cold," says Derek,
clamping his hands under his arms.

"May we have the bucket?" I ask.
"Chaps, everyone lean to this side."
The grown-ups join in.
We tilt the boat a bit,
and pool the water
into the bucket,
and toss it overboard.
There!
It's working!
We've almost got it all.

Then a big wave slops over the side—
*WHOOSH!*—

and drenched to the bone,
we have to start again.


## Our Poor Feet

The salt water eats at our feet.
Derek, Billy, and I are
lucky to have shoes.
Paul's in sandals;

Fred and Howard are barefoot.
My feet are cramped with cold,
but theirs turn white,
then red,
then blue.
They shrivel as they do
with too much time
in the bath.

"Look at these boys!"
yells Gunner Peard,
picking his way down the boat.
"Poor little rotters!"
Shouting and cursing
about women who don't know about children
and men who pray too much,
Peard wraps a blanket
around Paul's, Fred's, and Howard's feet.
They gaze up at him, astonished.
                Peard is bad-mannered and bossy,
                but he gets the job done.

## Passing the Time

"Did you want to go?"
Paul asks.

"I jolly well did!" says Howard, a proper London lad.
"My parents warned me about torpedoes,

but I wanted to see a ship
and meet real Navy men."

Huh. No one warned me about torpedoes.
"I was over the moon to go," says Fred.
"I couldn't wait to ship out
but my mum kept hanging on to me.
It was like trying to get away
from an octopus.
Even my Dad
had a few tears in his eyes.
But I couldn't wait. . . ."
No octopus hugs for me.

"My mum said we had to go
because we are part Jewish,"
says Derek.
"One of my great-grandmothers
ran off with a Jewish sailor, I think.
The Germans hate anyone
with a Jewish connection, you know.
Don't know why.
Mum cried
when we said good-bye. . . ."
No tears from mine. . . .

"My parents made me go," I say.
"My stepmum finally figured out
a way to get rid of me. . . ."
The boys look up, startled,

searching for something to say.
I change the subject.
"What about you, Paul?
Did you want to go?"
"I begged my parents
to go to Canada," he says,
"to get away from
the bullies at school.
I got the application myself
and had my sister
talk my mother into it.
My brother was going to go, too,
but he chickened out.
I say, why stop in Canada?
Why not sail the world?"

"You want to live on a ship?" I ask.

"I don't think so!" says Fred.
"Remember when
we were seasick on the ship?
Remember when
the torpedo hit, Paul?
I had to wake you up!
He sleeps through anything."

Paul looks down and studies the cut on his foot.

## A Tender Touch

I look up at the sky
and wonder
if my mum who died
is there in heaven
watching over us.
My hands and legs
start to tingle with pain,
numb from cramped quarters
and the cold.
"*Oi*, it prickles and burns!"

"Ken dear, let me rub your hands and feet,"
says Miss Cornish with a kind smile.
"It will help get
your circulation going."
I stiffen and blush with awkwardness
at her touch,
this lady I barely know,
but she's so gentle,
and her hands so warm.

I soon feel better.
She moves on to the next boy.
Her eyes look tired,
but she keeps working
to make sure we're all okay.

Miss Cornish doesn't have any children,
but she would make a good mother.

## Chins Up, Everyone!

Harry Peard
has seen enough of
sadness and hurt.
He picks his way
to the bow,
belting out naughty sea chanteys
to make us laugh.

Miss Cornish scowls
in disapproval,
but Peard gives us a grin.
"No use sulking, boys!" he shouts,
standing up,
stripping down to his shorts.
Miss Cornish turns away.
With a stretch and a leap,
he's over the side!

He's down, he's gone!

With a gasp,
we grasp the rails
and lean over,
looking for him.

"Where'd he go?" I shout.

His head pops up,
sputtering, laughing.
He's gone for a swim!

"Why are you going swimming, mister?"
asks Howard.

"To keep in practice,
in case we get torpedoed again,"
says Peard with a wink.

"He's a proper screwball, he is!"
says Fred with delight.

"Come on in, lads," he calls.

"I love swimming!" I say.

"Ignore the man," says Miss Cornish.

I can tell the adults
think Peard is mad.
He climbs aboard, laughing,
rocking the boat.

I think he's grand,
simply grand.

# Tension

Mary Cornish frowns
at Harry Peard,
dripping water in the boat.
He glances at us and scowls back at her.

"I hear you're just a piano teacher," he says.
"Now my wife,
she's got a way with kids, she has.
Keeps 'em fit as fleas,
and stands no nonsense neither."

I look at Miss Cornish.
Uh-oh. I see her pull herself up,
but Peard won't stop.

"What do you know about kids?
Got none of your own,
nor likely to have either."

"You're right on both counts," says Miss Cornish,
staring back with her wise brown eyes,
tucking her dark hair back
with her slender white hands.
"And what of it?"

They stare at each other
for a few seconds.

"No offense, of course,"
says Peard, finding his way
back to his seat.
We boys look at each other,
surprised to hear adults having a row,
allowing children to hear.

Harry mutters about Miss Cornish,
but she rubs our cold feet,
asks us questions,
suggests a song. . . .

*"There'll Always Be an England,"* says Derek.
And we sing that there will be.

*"Pack Up Your Troubles in Your Old Kit Bag,"* I say.
It does us all good singing
to pass the time.

*"What's the use of worrying,*
*it never was worthwhile.*
*So pack up your troubles in your old kit bag,*
*and smile, smile, smile."*

Yes, Peard calls Mary "spinster"
under his breath,
with scorn in his voice,
but we boys call her Auntie Mary
because she takes care of us.

# The Loo

What do you do
when there is no loo?
No privacy
and nothing to do
but pee over the side.

I learn the shipboard wisdom
of not pissing into the wind.

And there is a bucket
passed down from hand to hand.

"Who needs it now?"
ask the sailors,
busy with bailing.
"*Memsahib!*" say the crewmen.

We boys circle Auntie Mary,
facing away,
when it is her turn.
She takes care of us
and we take care of her.

## Raise a Flag

"We need a flag," Cooper says,
"in case we see a ship or a plane.
We need something to wave,
to send a signal,
to save us all."

There is no flag.

Auntie Mary turns,
slips inside her jacket
and thin silk blouse,
and pulls out her chemise.
"Use this," she says.

The boys and I stifle snorts
and the men turn as pink
as our new flag,
but Signalman Mayhew
shinnies up the mast
and ties it to the top.

Rally round the flag, boys!
Our small pink flag!

Harry Peard's open mouth closes.
"Well, I'll be . . . ," he says.

## Sardines?

At six o'clock,
our first supper
of our long day one
comes down the line—
another ship's biscuit,
a sardine,
another dipperful of water,
a tin of condensed milk
shared by six.
The milk is sweet,
but it makes us thirstier.
And I hate sardines.
*Yech!*
But I'm hungry.
                    So hungry.

We say grace
before and after our meal.
"Father," I say,
"the prayer
lasts longer
than the meal itself."

## Questions

After supper,
we face a second long night

aboard Lifeboat 12.

It's cold, bloomin' cold.
I shiver under my wet coat
and stare out at the waves,
rocked by the questions
in my head.
Where is the Navy?
Where is our rescue?
They should be here by now.

Have the other lifeboats been rescued?
Are the survivors warm and dry, eating hot soup?
Do my parents know what happened to us?

Does anyone?

## God Is Wise

I hear Ramjam Buxoo,
talking with Father O'Sullivan.

"Allah the Compassionate
will save us
if He so wishes.
Or
He will send storms
if He thinks it best.
God is wise."

Father O'Sullivan closes his eyes
and clasps his hands together.
"Hail Mary, full of Grace. . . ."

And it's only by the grace of God,
I sleep.

## Routine, Ritual, and Risk

Daylight brings stretching,
prayers,
no breakfast,
a quick wash.
I dry my face with
Mr. Nagorski's newspaper
and borrow Cadet Critchley's comb.
I help the sailors stand watch,
hoping to spot a plane,
a ship on the horizon.

I notice most Indian sailors rinse their mouths
along with their faces.
"Why do they do that?" I ask Father O'Sullivan.
"It's a religious ritual they perform
before they pray," says Father.

"Aren't they afraid they'll swallow the seawater?"

"Yes, they have to be careful."

But as I watch, I see one man
who doesn't spit the water out.
I see him swallow. . . .


## Time Stretches Out

Officer Cooper
and Father O'Sullivan
synchronize their wristwatches—
the only two on board.

Time stretches
ahead of us,
hours of floating
to the distant horizon
with not much to do,
hours and hours
of endless time
until we remember
we have only
seven days of water left.

                                   Time is running out.


## Pushing On

"Right!" says Cooper.
"Time for a new plan.

We are going to make for Ireland."

"What about waiting
for the rescue ship?"
asks Mr. Nagorski.

"It must have missed us somehow,"
says Cooper.

Auntie Mary looks alarmed
and Howard starts to cry.
"How shall we get home?"
he asks.

"Chins up," says Cooper.
"The current
has been pushing us east,
pushing us to shore
all this time.
Now we'll help it along.
Buxoo, have your crew
man the Fleming gear!"

I look at Cooper's face,
steady with determination.
If we aren't going
to be picked up one way
we are going to get to Ireland.
Nobody has the slightest intention
of ever giving up hope. No.

It's up to us to save ourselves.
We're going to row home.
Maximum speed?
Two to three knots.
But with Fleming gear
anyone can row,
You just
push, pull
      push, pull
            push, pull.

## Wind

With flattening seas,
this stiff westerly wind
could whisk us along.

"Too rough before," says Cooper,
"but now we can sail."
Purvis frees the canvas,
rolled up under the floorboards.
Cooper hoists it high.

I've never been on a sailboat before.
It's lovely the way
the wind allows
my friends and me to sit back,
breathe out,
and watch the sail

billow and fill,
blowing us home.


## The Hole

"Did you see the hole
the torpedo blew
in the ship?" I ask.
"Did you see the hole
by the playroom?"

"Without a lie,
you could have put
two double-decker buses
in it!" says Fred.

Derek and Billy,
holes in their hearts,
ask again
about their little brothers.

"I shared a bunk bed
with Alan at home," says Derek.
"I'd read to him
and he would read back to me.
He could tie his shoelaces
and he's only five."

"Peter's just a wee bairn

and he's aye gettin' lost,"
says Billy.
"I promised Maw. . . ."

Father O'Sullivan
puts his arms
around their shoulders
and whispers a prayer.
Billy stares at the floorboards
and starts to choke.
I reach over to pat his back.

Where are their brothers?
No one,
not even Father O'Sullivan,
has any answers.


## Afternoon Routine

Lunch at noon,
Peard swimming when the sea is calm,
sailors plotting our course,
manning the Fleming gear when the wind dies,
standing watch.
Dinner at six.

But for us boys,
there is nothing to do.
At least Robinson Crusoe

had a shelter to build,
food to hunt,
clothes to sew,
sheep to raise,
paper and ink to write.
For us,
there's nothing to occupy our time,
nothing to see but the sea—
an ocean of gray,
melting into mist
that rises to the steely sky.
There's nothing to break
the horizon
or the rows of relentless waves
marching us to the ends of the earth.

## Man Our Stations!

One look at our faces
and Critchley says,
"Right! You boys, we need your help!
You can man the Fleming gear."
"I know how," I say.

I show the others
and we take turns
pushing and pulling.
At least the exercise keeps us warm.
We help bail the boat

and stand on watch just like proper sailors.

I scan the horizon,
search the seas and skies
for a ship
or a seaplane I recognize
from my plane spotter's guide.

I sketch a warship
in the drops of salt water
dotting the deck.
Terry would draw it
better than I do.

We would make a good team,
Terry and I,
here on watch.

## Which Would You Rather Be?

"Bombed at home,
or torpedoed at sea?"
I ask Auntie Mary,
then turn it into a game
we play
for something to do,
something to say.

I ask each boy in turn.

"Not bombed at home!" says Derek.
"Torpedoed at sea!" says Billy.
"Torpedoed at sea," we all agree.
Just wait till we tell the lads at home.
What a story this will be!

## Pain

Paul is silent,
staring,
suffering.
"How is your foot, Paul?" I ask.
He cut his heel
on broken glass in his cabin
when the torpedo hit.
"It hurts so much," he says.
"The salt water stings."

He takes his sandals off.
"They're just too tight," he says.
I see his feet have swollen
and leak stinking pus from open sores.
I cover my nose and turn away.

"Trench foot," whispers Father O'Sullivan
to Auntie Mary.

My shoes feel tight now.
I loosen the laces

and see my feet are swelling.
Will I get trench foot?

I shudder.
Too much water on our feet,
not enough down our throats. . . .

## Remember?

"Remember the water
in our cabins?" asks Derek.
"The water in a carafe,
changed every day?
I remember trying the water
and it was so good,
nice chilled water."

Water.
A whole carafe
of clear . . . fresh . . . clean . . . water.
"I'd trade my bike
for just one glass of water," I say.

"I'd trade my shrapnel collection," says Derek.

"I'd give me go-cart," says Billy.

"Boys, boys," says Auntie Mary,
quickly placing a hand

on Billy's arm.
"How about a game?"


# I Spy

"You know that game, don't you?"
says Mary. "Derek, you go first."
"I spy something white," he says.
"The sail?"
"The cloud?"
"The crew's tunics?"
"Your buttons!"
"Right, Fred. Now you go."

"I spy . . . um . . . I spy. . . ."
Fred looks all around
and suddenly stops.
He whispers, "I spy someone crying. . . ."
It's Paul.
He looks up and winces.
"My feet. They hurt so much."

"Let me help you,"
says Mary, moving over to
put her arm around Paul.
"You boys keep playing.
Ken, you take a turn."
I spy cold, wet boys,
Father O'Sullivan feverish, seasick,

praying crewmen,
worried looks between officers.
I don't want to play anymore.

Throats dry,
glassy-eyed,
we slump to the floorboards and stare
unseeing. . . .

## We May Die

Auntie Mary looks from face to face
and stops at mine.
"Ken, are you all right?" she asks.
I look up into her warm brown eyes.

Auntie Mary sees what I see.
She realizes we may die—
not of hunger
not of thirst
not of exhaustion—
not yet anyway.
It sounds odd to say
but it's true,
we may die of the doldrums
as the days drift by.

"How about a story?" she says.
"It's called . . .

## The Case of the Kidnapped Pilots

Six boys were riding their bikes in the English countryside when a British plane roared over the coast with a Luftwaffe fighter plane on its tail. The aircraft swooped and dove while the sound of machine gunfire filled the air high above the boys' heads.

*Rat-a-tat, tat, tat!* Then *BOOM!*

The Brit was hit! A parachute floated down as the plane spiraled to the ground. *CRASH!*

The boys raced down the road, following the trail of smoke.

"Look!" said Ken. "There's the pilot. He's still alive."

The pilot was bleeding badly. Howard tore off his shirt, ripped it into pieces, and tied tourniquets above the man's wounds. The pilot muttered, "The pouch, get the pouch. . . ."

Paul found it in the folds of the parachute.

"Take care of him," said Ken. "I'll go get help."

He strapped the pouch across his chest and scrambled onto his bike. Ken had a friend who lived nearby, a piano teacher named Mary. "She'll know what to do," he thought.

One look at the courier pouch and Mary picked up the phone. "This," she said, "is a job for Bulldog Drummond!"

"BULLDOG?" I say.
We all know about Bulldog—
the hero of dozens of British books and films
who always beats the scoundrels.

Auntie Mary smiles, folds her hands,
and says, "That's all for today."

"Come on, don't stop," I say.
"Mary, please?" says Paul.

But Mary means what she says
and can't be persuaded otherwise.
I see a small smile on her lips.
Thanks to her,
I see we now have something
to think about,
something besides
hunger,
thirst,

and cold.
As the misty air clears
and the red sun sets,
a double rainbow arcs over us.
All the colors of the world
lighten and
brighten
our day.

Just as Bulldog has.

## Chills

Cold, so cold,
we shiver together,
wrapped in two blankets
for the six of us.

The temperature has plunged
since yesterday.
Chunks of ice
the sailors call growlers
float by.

It grows dark,
but it's hard to sleep
crumpled in
the bottom of the boat
with the thwarts

in your back.
I close my eyes
and just as I start to doze off—
*whoosh!*
A wall of ice-cold water
washes over the side,
soaking us all.
I sit up choking,
spluttering,
wiping the salt
from my eyes.

The blanket is soaked,
stone cold.
I can't stop shaking.

In the dark,
someone whimpers.

I can't see who it is,
but I hear Auntie Mary whisper,
"Don't you realize
that you're the heroes
of a real adventure story?"

"There isn't a boy in England
who wouldn't give his eyes
to be in your shoes!"

"Did you ever hear of a hero who sniveled?"

Right she is.
Bulldog Drummond would never snivel.

And just like that
the sniveling stops.
The stars whirl in the sky
and I sleep.

## The Millionaire

We wake to
shimmering sun.
"Hey, mister, what are you doing?"
I ask Mr. Nagorski,
who sits just behind us with the escorts.
The businessman smiles at me
as he pulls out his money,
pound note upon note,
laying them on the floorboards.
"Drying things out!" he says.

"You must be rich, huh?"
"I think he's a count," whispers Paul.
"I think he's a diplomat," whispers Fred.
"I work in shipping," he says.
"My wife and daughters are waiting
for me in Canada."

He seems a kind lot,
this tall gentleman
with kid gloves,

a homburg hat,
and a fur coat he shares with us
to keep our feet warm.

I watch his bills curl in the sun.
Hey, that reminds me!
What happened to *my* money?
I gave it to our escorts
on the ship—
we all did—
and now?
"Where's OUR money, Mary?"
The awful realization hits me.
"Now it's at the bottom of the sea, isn't it?"

"I'm afraid so," admits Mary.

"What!"

"Oh, Mary, I had thirteen bob!
More than half a pound!"

"My parents can never replace that money!"

"Crikey, it was all I had!"

The kind gentleman
in the homburg hat says,
"Listen, lads, I will replace your money
when we get home."

Could he mean it?
I think he does.
I thank him,
stunned by his generosity.
From then on,
we call him The Millionaire.

Thanks to him,
we'll have a story to tell
*and* all our money
when we get home.

## Hard to Swallow

Three days in the lifeboat
and my throat
is so dry
I can no longer swallow
the hard ship's biscuit
that comes with our
sardine or salmon at lunchtime.
I have no saliva
to wash it down.

"These biscuits are so hard,"
says Fred. "I reckon you could
mend the boat with them if you got holed."
He tosses his overboard.

I can't eat,
so I give my biscuit
to Auntie Mary
to hold for me.

But oh, how we eye
the water ration!
All of us boys sit up
and lick our lips
as the little cup
comes down the line.
Lord help the fool
who spills a drop!
When it's my turn,
I even lick the string
attached to the cup
so as not to waste
a precious drop.

There are six days of water left.
Drink! Drink!
It's all we can think. . . .

## Trench Foot

Meanwhile the salt water
eats away at my feet.
We boys are all barefoot now
because our shoes are too tight.

As time goes by,
my feet shrink,
then swell,
stink,
turn into blisters
and open sores.
    My stomach turns
looking at them.

Paul's feet are the worst.
The skin is turning black.
Will mine too?
    Rot and decay
    washes over us with each wave
    and starts to seep inside. . . .


## Suffering

Most of the crewmen from India
are barefoot too.
They only have thin
cotton clothing.
They must be frozen to death.

"Why don't they have
warmer clothes, Father?" I ask.

"They came from India,
stopped in Liverpool,

and were expecting
a return trip home," he says.
"They weren't expecting
to come out toward the Atlantic."

"They're used to a hot country
and the cold North Atlantic
isn't anybody's fun," says Fred.

Here on the lifeboat,
they may be suffering the most.

They were so kind to me
on the ship.
I recognize many of them
from the dining room
and realize
they aren't seamen,
but stewards,
as unprepared
as I am to face
this heartless sea.
Wrapped in blankets,
they are restless,
shivering,
teeth chattering.
They talk ceaselessly
in a language
I can't understand.

Sure, the stewards
know English words for food,
but talk of food isn't much use here.

I watch the man with the little mustache,
the one who smiled at me.

He can't avoid
the water that pools
in the center of the boat.
His feet are as swollen as Paul's.
His smile is a grimace now.

## Losing Hope

My friend prays to Allah,
and like many of his fellow crewmen,
bows to the east five times a day.

"What are they doing?" I ask Father.
"Bowing to Mecca," he says,
"the holy city of Islam.
It's where Muhammad the Prophet was born."

I notice other crewmen
crossing themselves as Father does.

"Some of the men
are from Goa," explains Father.

"They're Catholic, like me."

Despite the different prayers,
I see many of the crewmen
are starting to give up hope.
"Don't do it!" I want to tell them.
"We'll be all right."

I sit up and shake down
a rising panic.
"We'll be all right!" I shout.
A few of the men look over,
startled at my outburst,
but most slump and stare,
growing listless.
And later, some collapse,
slipping into comas.

## Pack Up Your Troubles

How can I be so wet
when my throat is so dry?
How can I be sunburned
*and* frostbitten?
How can I be so exhausted
and unable to sleep?

That song we sang

about packing up your troubles
runs through my head.
I'd like to pack up my troubles
and throw them overboard.

I look at the younger boys whimpering,
and I know what we need.
"Auntie Mary," I say.
"Tell us more about Bulldog."
"Good idea," says Mary.
"Let's see, Ken had taken
the pilot's pouch to Mary and
she called Bulldog. . . .

Captain Hugh Drummond, alias Bulldog
Drummond, knocked on Mary's door. He was
six feet tall and no doubt his face had earned
him the nickname Bulldog. He was cheerfully
ugly, supremely self-confident in an expertly
tailored suit. He got right to business. "A
courier's pouch, you say?" he asked. "Right, let's
have a look." And in one trick move, he snapped
the lock and pulled out some papers. "They're
in code. That pilot should be in hospital by now.
I'll take the pouch and pay him a visit."

He stood to leave, but stopped at the newspaper
on Mary's table. "Great Scott," he said. "I
wonder, could this pouch have something to
do with those missing pilots?"

Mary and Ken hurried over to read the headline.

### ACE PILOTS MISSING!
### BRITAIN'S FINEST KIDNAPPED?

These three men were on leave and did not return," said their Squadron Leader James Bigglesworth. "But they're not the type to desert their posts. I suspect foul play.

Bulldog turned to Ken. "Well, young man, you and your friends saved one life today. And who knows, if these things are connected, we may save a few more."

At the hospital, Drummond found the injured pilot delirious, babbling nonsense about estates and elm trees. A nurse was taking notes on her chart. She stared at the pouch in Bulldog's hands and hurried away without a word.

Bulldog followed. He wasn't surprised when she dropped her nurse's hat and coat into a rubbish bin outside. "You're no Florence Nightingale, are you, old girl?" he muttered.

The woman hurried down the street, stopping every once in a while at a store window while glancing behind her. Satisfied that Bulldog was indeed following her, she ducked into a restaurant.

Through the window, Bulldog saw her join a
man who seemed familiar. In profile, he had
a sharp nose, a short dark beard, a stern but
strikingly elegant manner. He turned and
Bulldog knew him in an instant. Peterson!

"Peterson?"
gasped Howard.
"That snake!" said Billy.

"Yes," says Mary.
"It was Peterson,
Bulldog's arch enemy.
What will Bulldog do, boys?
What do you think?
We'll find out tomorrow."

"Oh, Mary," moans Fred.
Groans all around,
but we'll dream of
Bulldog tonight. . . .

### A Visitor

Father O'Sullivan spots it first.
"Look!" he calls, pointing to
a black shape rising in the water,
ten yards from our boat.

"A U-boat!" yells Fred,
panic in his voice.

            WHAT?
                    God help us!

"No," shouts Father,
pulling himself up on his feet
for the first time all week.
"It's a WHALE!"

I pop up
and Derek and Billy
are on their knees beside me,
pointing and shouting
as the slick black whale
ribbons in and out of the waves.
"Crikey, look!" I say.

"There's another! Whales!"

We kneel in awe,
watching the two
perform for us,
arching up, curling down,
twins in tandem
who surface and dive,
                          surface and dive.

One swims right up,
as if to say,
what are *you* doing here
in my waters?

Then, as suddenly
as the whales appeared,
heave ho—
there they go.

Later that day, the colors
of the western sky collide,
mirrored in the east
as if we are watching
two sunsets at once.

Even the sailors had never
seen such a phenomenon.
We sit smiling at each other,
grateful for diversion,

even for just a little while
as we listen
to the priest's prayer of thanks
for sunsets,
for whales,
for the marvels
of this world.


## A Good Day

Whales and a tale—
that's what good days
are made of.
I whisper to Mary,
"Please, may we have
more of the story now?"

"Yes, let's see, where were we?"
she says.

We all know—
"At the restaurant with Peterson!"

Yes, it was Peterson, and as usual, he was up
to no good. Bulldog nipped into the restaurant
unnoticed, determined to find out what this
ah . . . snake as you so rightly call him . . . had to
do with the pilot and the coded papers.

"Yes, sir?" asked the waiter.

"A sarsaparilla, my good man," said Bulldog. "On duty, you know."

"Jolly good, sir."

Ten minutes later, Peterson and the woman left the restaurant through a back door. Bulldog tailed them into the alley.

But Peterson was waiting for him. "Ah, Captain Drummond, we meet again!" he said.

"Well, well, Peterson," said Bulldog. "If I know you, and I do, I suspect you're up to something. You and your . . . ah . . . nurse."

Peterson just smiled as he stepped up to his cream-colored Rolls-Royce. "No time, old man. Just hand over that pouch and I'll be off. Business meeting with a chap I'm going to convince to break this code for me. People pay millions for codes, don't they?"

"Stop!" said Bulldog, but his vision blurred. He took a step and stumbled.

"Hope you enjoyed your sarsaparilla," said Peterson, snatching the pouch. Drummond realized his drink had been drugged. He sank to his knees and fell onto the pavement.

Three boys on their bikes passed the alleyway
in time to see Bulldog slump to the ground
and hear Peterson direct his driver, "The Elms
Estate and be quick about it!"

"Peterson got away?"
asks Fred.

"And Bulldog is dead,
isn't he?" says Paul.

"Of course not," I tell him.
"Heroes can't die.
Then there'd be no story."

                  And we can't face that.

# SUNDAY, 22 SEPTEMBER

## 4 DAYS OF WATER LEFT

### Rain!

Not mist this time,
but real fat drops of
falling-down rain!
Like baby birds,
we open our mouths
and stretch our throats
upward to the skies.

"Quick! Let's try to catch the rainwater!"
yells Cooper. "Spread the sail!"
The officers and crew
grab the ends of the sail
and stretch it out
to collect the drops.
My throat catches
at the thought of
extra water,
blessed water to drink!

The rain
pools and puddles

on the sail
and for a good ten minutes
we and the sailors channel it
into the empty milk cans
from our rations.

"Here, boys, share this one,"
says Purvis.
He passes the precious can
to Billy, who takes the first drink.

*"Agh!"* he says, choking.
"It's salty."

"Don't swallow!" says Purvis.

"Spit it out," says Cooper.
"The water must have
absorbed the salt
on the sail.
Don't drink it! It can kill you!"

All we can do is open
our mouths to catch
a spattering of luscious drops.

But then the rain slows
                              and stops.

## Feeling Low

That was a blow
to think
that we might have extra water
for our salt-caked lips
and our tongues
hanging heavy
in our mouths
like dying fish flopping
on dry land.

## A Treat

"Never mind," says Georgy Porgy.
"Today we will have a treat."
Along with our sardine,
and dipperful of water,
we will have dessert—
a peach!
Well, not a peach,
not half a peach,
but a slice of canned peach
for each boy.
Georgy Porgy passes them down.
And OH,
the joy of it!
A smooth, silky
slide of sweetness,

succulent
and tantalizing.
"It's like candy, is what it is," says Fred.
A brief mouthwatering moment,
and then it is gone.

But nothing has ever tasted that good.

## Where's Bulldog?

"Bulldog didn't die,
did he?" asks Fred.

"No, the boys will save him,"
I say. "They call Mary."

"Right," says Derek.
"She gets him home,
gives him tea,
and soon he's right as rain."

"Tea." Mary sighs. "Rain.
Oh, boys, what I wouldn't give for . . .
oh, never mind, let's get on with our story. . . ."

Mary tended to Bulldog's bruises as they
listened to the wireless for news of the missing
pilots. There was news—the pilot in the
hospital had disappeared! "And I have no idea

where Peterson has gone," said Bulldog.

"Does the Elms Estate mean anything to you? The boys overheard Peterson say that to his driver," said Mary.

"Ah, good lads, I know the place," said Bulldog. "I'll go as soon as it's dark."

Black shadows had fallen when Bulldog sneaked onto the grounds. Only a single candle flickered in a window. *"AGHH!"* someone screamed. Bulldog ducked beneath the window and saw Peterson interrogating a prisoner. The man was bent over in pain, a torture device called a thumbscrew beside the coded papers on the table. "Give me the key to these codes or I'll go to work on your other hand," said Peterson.

Bulldog had to act. With one move, he crashed through the window and knocked over the candle. In the confusion, Bulldog landed a punch; Peterson went down. Bulldog slung the prisoner over his shoulder, grabbed the papers, and ran through the door into the night. The candle on the floor ignited the drapes and. . . .

## Smoke!

I see it first.
"Look, SMOKE!" I cry,
leaning out over the gunwale
and pointing to the horizon.

"He's right!" yells Critchley.
Far off, across the western horizon,
a dark spire
whorls in the wind.

It gets larger and larger
and soon a gray shape
appears beneath it,
breaking the line of the horizon.
Is it land?
No.
It's getting bigger.
Is it a ship?
I think it IS a ship!
Will it see us?

It's coming closer!
My God, it is a ship!

The mast and funnels
are soon in view.
"It's a merchant ship!" says Cooper.
"Shoot off the flares!"

*Whoosh! Whoosh!*
Flaming shots
rocket high
into the sky.
The sailors wave their arms
and shout.


"Boys, we must pray,"
says Father O'Sullivan.
"Come now, we must help the Lord
lead that ship this way."
He kneels
and reluctantly we do too,
peeking at the horizon as we say
the Lord's Prayer together.
"Thank you, God," I whisper.
"Thank you for sending us a ship.
Please, please, please, let it see us."
I glance up.
"LOOK!" I shout, interrupting the prayer.
The boys and I scramble to our feet.
"LOOK!
           IT'S TURNING!
                     IT'S COMING THIS WAY!"


"You're right, Ken!" says Cooper.
"Looks like she's seen us!"


I turn to Mary
and hug her hard

as gleeful shouts
        ring out!


"They've seen us!"            *"Allah!"*


            "They're coming!"
"Hallelujah!"


            "Thanks be to God!"


                    "We're going home!"


The ship is about two miles away.
Then one.
Soon they are not more
than seven hundred yards away!
Great God, we are saved!

Amid hugging and cheering,
I think of what this means.
We'll have water and food and warm clothes and a bed.
We're going home.
Just wait till my friends
hear of our adventure,
of all we survived!
                    WE ARE SAVED!

## Prepare for Rescue

Captain's orders:
"Trim the sail.
Prepare for rescue.
Bring down the awning.
Throw those supports overboard—
they're just in the way."

The crew cheers,
rejoicing in rescue,
as we all get ready
to greet
the ship.
Here it comes,
closer and closer,
it's almost here,
but
      WAIT!
          What is happening?

Cooper stands stock-still.
Mayhew waves frantically.
Critchley bends over
and grasps his knees,
breathing hard.
I look at the ship,
at our officers,
and back at the ship.
A sob escapes my throat.

Billy and Fred whimper
and reach for Mary,
who crushes them to her.
Paul just stares as
Father O'Sullivan collapses.

What is happening?

**NO!**


# The Ship Has Turned

Our dreams of being saved,
our happy endings,
are scuttled
as the ship turns again
away from us
and pushes north.

It grows smaller
and smaller
and dipping down below the horizon,
is gone.

Why did they turn?

Where are they going?

How could they leave us?

What's the use in praying?

Too many questions
rush into my head,
swamping my thoughts—
dead weights
pushing me under.
I can't breathe.

Night is falling and
a mass of black clouds gathers
in the ship's wake.
We are in for another storm.

For the first time,
I can't see my way home.

My friends and I
break down,
all but Paul,
who is so weak
he has no tears left to cry.

## Forsaken

Father O'Sullivan
is bowed and shaken.
He clasps his hands together.
*"Thy kingdom come,*
*Thy will be done. . . ."*

## No Sulking, See!

After a time,
gruff old Gunner Peard
picks his way up to the bow.
"What's the matter now?"
he demands to know.
"Down-'earted 'cos she didn't pick us up?
*That's* nothing to worry about."

I stare up at him
through my tears.
Is he mad?
"We'll see plenty more ships tomorrow
now we've reached the sea lanes," he says.

"Sea lanes?"

"It's where all the ships pass through,
he says. "There'll be another soon enough."

I have to believe him.
"That's right," I tell my friends.
"If Peard says so.
It must be true."

                             It has to be.

## The Tempest

That night,
chilling clouds
collide
and split,
spilling rain,
spitting hail,
slashing sideways.

I open my mouth
to sweet cold rain,
but a wave
force-feeds me
a mouthful
of salt instead.

Spitting and gagging,
I wipe my mouth
and just try to hold on.

Bitter winds
whip the waves into
twenty-foot towers.
Our boat surfs up each crest,
flies off the top—
then slams twenty feet down,
stinging spray,
soaking us through.

Lightning bolts
fire jagged daggers.
Fear
like none I've felt before
flashes through me,
fed by the crash
of thunder.

I grip the rails,
white knuckled,
wondering,
will we survive this night?
Billy and Paul look at me
        wild-eyed with panic.

                "Hold on, hold on," I shout.
                    "You've got to hold on!"

## We Are Alive

In the light,
bodies are still,
alive,
but nearly paralyzed
with exhaustion.
We are bruised and beaten
and cannot eat.
My throat is raw with sores,
my tongue and mouth
sucked dry to the bone.

My friends are whimpering.
Enough.
                    ENOUGH!
                              We want to go home.


## Suck Your Buttons

That's what Gunner Peard says,
"If you're thirsty,

suck yer buttons
to get yer saliva goin'."

Derek has a Lamb of God charm
that Father O'Sullivan gave him.
He wears it round his neck,
so he sucks on that.
With a sad smile, he jokes,
"Look at me!
I'm the only
bloke on the boat
having leg of lamb."

## An Idea

Father O'Sullivan
pulls out a safety pin
and a bit of string from his pocket.
He bends the safety pin into a hook
and ties it to the string.

"What are you making, Father?"
I ask.

"I'm sick of sardines,
so with luck,
I'm going to catch us
something different for dinner," he says,
nodding to the seagulls

landing on the water nearby.

"Blimey! NO, man!" cries Peard.
"Harming a seabird
is bad luck, is what it is.
Don't you know?
They carry the souls
of dead sailors.
Kill one and
it'll be an albatross
around all our necks!"

"We have plenty of sardines,"
says Purvis. "No use
risking bad luck."

I look out at the seagulls
that swim for a bit,
then just flap their wings
to soar over our heads
and fly away home.

If only a wizard
would turn me into a gull
the way Merlyn turned Wart into an owl. . . .
I would fly away home.

Magic or no magic,
luck or no luck,
seagulls are a sign

that land
may be near.


## Look!

Cooper shouts and points.
The sailors who are able
rouse themselves
and turn to look in that direction.
I sit up and peer
off in the distance,
squinting hard.
My head hurts
and I start to shiver uncontrollably.
Auntie Mary wraps an arm
around me
and feels my forehead.
I pull away
because suddenly
I see what Cooper sees.
A charcoal mass
floats on the horizon.
What is THAT?
I stare
as it teases and taunts.
Could it be?
Could it be?
Dear God, could it be . . .

*LAND?*

## Light the Way

"Steer that way!" orders Cooper.
Mayhew trims the sail
and we steer toward the strange shape
so far away.
We sail all day,
as I drift in and out of sleep.
I wake as the sun sets.
Mary looks at me
with concern in her eyes,
says something I cannot hear.
Night drops down,
clouds shrouding the stars.
The stars!
I remember we have no compass.
How will we stay on course
if we can't see the stars?

I'm cold, bitter cold,
but my head feels hot,
blasted hot
like the last handheld flare
our captain ties to the top
of the mast.
If it IS land, maybe
someone will see us.

The flare casts an eerie red glow
on the bodies below,

its flash reflected
by the tiny fish—
phosphorescence—
in the water.
Hope flames
in my head tonight.


## Delirious

Hope!

HELP!

No, don't . . .

I want . . .

I can't. . . .

Help them!


They're tipping!

So many swimming and sinking

slipping and surfacing

sliding under . . .

BULLDOG!

I can't get to them!

Terry!

Dad!

Margaret!

Mum!

I can't get there!

hope

HELP!

## Smoke and Mirrors

I wake from a fitful sleep,
weary, confused.
I dreamed I was falling,
falling off the ship!

"Are you all right, now, Ken?"
asks Mary, eyes poring into me
as she rubs my sore, stiff legs.

Now I remember!
"We saw land, Mary! LAND!
Remember?"
I swivel my head in all directions.

She doesn't answer.

"Mary!" I say. "Tell me!"

"There is no land, Ken,"
says Mary softly.
"It was the clouds,
a mirage."

And just like that—
*poof!*—
the promise of land
disappears into thin air.
The clouds and sea
are smoke and mirrors,
evil magicians
hypnotizing us,
conjuring land,
hope,
home
with hocus-pocus.
Cruel con artists.
There is no land.
        Hope is a hoax.

And now the waves,
glittering like knives,
take aim at us,
our backs
against the wall.

We grit our teeth,
face each roller as it hits
and slice through,
bracing ourselves
till the next wave hits.

        There are two days of water left.

## No More!

After a time,
the waves subside,
slowing their cruel ride.
The wind whistles,
indifferent to what it's done.

I try to sit up
and unstick my tongue
from the roof
of my dry-as-dust mouth.
My eyes sting
from the salt water
that washed over us.

I notice Ramjam Buxoo
checking the breathing
of a few of his crewmen,
including the young mustached man
who had smiled at me.
Is he all right?
Is he alive?

Suddenly,
a crewman stands,
the one I saw
swallowing the seawater.
I don't know his name.
I don't understand

what he's shouting.

The other crewmen
look startled or annoyed.

He strips,
and arms up,
shouts to the sky.
Then, to my astonishment,
he springs over the side.

He bobs up,
torture on his face.
"He can't swim," I yell. "He's sinking!"
"Help him!" Mary screams.

We boys and his fellow crewmen
jump up, rocking the boat.
Buxoo, Cooper, and Critchley
reach for him,
but the waves whisk him away.
He surfaces again,
coughing and calling,
but he's too far gone.

He swings his arms,
bobbing and weaving,
fighting the waves.
But with a one-two punch
from the sea,

he goes down,
for the last time.

I slump down, stunned.
I've never seen a man drown before.
Wailing floods the boat.

Paul ducks under the canvas cover
as Father starts to pray.

"He went mad, boys,"
whispers Auntie Mary,
staring straight ahead.
"He lost his mind."

The man is no more.

## First Aid

I see the crew
is unmoored.
I see the sores
on their feet
and the suffering
on their faces.

I watch Buxoo move
from man to man
in his crew,

whispering,
reassuring them.

I ask Father O'Sullivan,
"What can I do?"

Father is too weak to stand,
but my question rouses him.
He nods at me
and says, "We've got to do something."
He whispers to
Mr. Nagorski,
who pulls out
a small
bottle of medicine
from the first aid kit.

Mr. Nagorski
anoints the feet
of the crewmen
whose sores are open wounds.
Buxoo explains
that the medicine
will ease their pain
and leads them in prayer.

There is no remedy
for what has happened,
only small relief.

Nagorski moves to each one in turn,
and I see how
one small kindness between strangers
offers distraction
from Death,
who now occupies
that empty seat on our boat.


## Fading Fast

Sunburned,
windburned,
I am scorched
and now
the fire is dying.
I look around and see
the gleam in our eyes,
the spark inside us all
is flickering,
fading
to
cold
gray
ash.

## I Have One Question

"What is Bulldog doing?
Please, Auntie Mary," I beg.
"Please."

"Yes, darling."
And struggling to speak,
she begins again.

## Bulldog, Continued

"Bulldog is at home,
sitting in my . . . ah, his
big red easy chair,"
whispers Mary.
"He's wearing his slippers,
sipping a hot drink,
in front of a crackling fire."
She shivers as she leans back
and closes her eyes.

"But wha' aboot th' man he rescued
from Peterson's thumbscrews , Mary?"
Billy asks.

"What *happened?*" says Howard.
"Where are the missing pilots?
Did Bulldog crack the codes?"

"Cracked the codes," says Mary.
"All is well."

"But HOW?" asks Derek.
"What did the codes say?
Mary, please tell us!"

Mary sits up and opens her eyes.
She looks at me,
and then the younger boys
one by one,
seeing we are all starved,
starved for our story.

She coughs and whispers . . .

The man Bulldog rescued decoded the pilot's
papers. Um, there was something about a spy,
yes, a spy for the Germans. His name was, ah,
Cage, John Cage. He owned a pub—the Ship's
Pub.

"Scotland Yard suspected
he was up to no good, right, Mary?"
I say trying to help her.
"He was hiding something. . . ."

"That's right," she says.
"He had the keys."

"The keys?" asks Paul.
"The keys to what?"

"The keys to everything. . . . ,"
says Mary, drifting off to sleep.


## Madness

Tonight,
screaming scares me awake.
I rub my eyes, confused.

"Drink . . .
give me a drink . . .
I am going mad!"

It's Paul.
His feet have swelled even more.
They're double in size.

"Help me!" screams Paul.

"His feet,"
whispers Father O'Sullivan
to Auntie Mary. "They're much worse."
Paul screams when Mary touches them.

"It's okay, Paul," I say,
patting his arm.

He turns, looks me in the eye,
and howls,
"I am MAD!
Water!"

The officers exchange
grim glances.
We all want water.
We all need water.

Craving and fear
rock the boat,
but Paul's screams
may sink us all.

Father O'Sullivan
whispers in French
with Mr. Nagorski.
I hear *"il va mourir. . . ."*
It is decided.
Critchley stands
and quietly
delivers a dipper of water.
Mutinous eyes follow him
from stern to bow.
Envy rises in me,
but I tell myself Paul needs the water more.

Paul is given enough
to moisten his lips,

but then he wants more!
MORE!

In the darkness,
I feel tense rustling and rumblings
coursing the length of the boat.
No one could sleep
through the screams.
Is Paul really going mad?
I look at the other boys,
eyes wide in the shadows.
Everyone needs the screaming to stop.

## Screams Interrupted

"What NOW?"
demands a loud voice in the dark.
It's Harry Peard, making his way
up to the bow.
"Water? Is *that* all?
Of course you want water.
We all do.
You'll get yer water in the mornin'!
Now you forget about it.
Is *that* all that's wrong with you?"

"My . . . my feet are cold," whimpers Paul.

"Critchley, give me your overcoat,"

says Peard.

He takes it and rewraps Paul's feet,
muttering all the while.

"Are yer feet warm now?" demands Peard.

"Y-y-yes. . . . ," says Paul.

Peard curses his way back to the stern
and Paul sleeps.

## Sunrise

We should be happy
on a day like this.
The rising sun
halos the eastern horizon,
reflecting a long yellow path
in the water
that leads back home.

Yes, we should be happy
on a day like this.
But we have one day of water left.

What we need is rain.

## Running on Empty

It's Day 8,
the day we should have reached Ireland,
the day we run out of water.

In a book,
this would be the climax of our story—
the point where all the drama happens,
where all the problems are solved,
where the happy ending begins.

This would be the day we are rescued.

I scan the horizon,
but
there is nothing,
nothing to break
the blues of sea and sky.

Purvis says there are
still stores of food.
But who can swallow it
without water
to wash it down?

He says the tank is low.
There will be
no
water
this lunch.

Silence fills the boat
as we drift,
all of us

blank and staring,
vacant shells
of the people we once were,
still
and empty as our tank.


## Islands Alone

I look up
and think of Earth
floating in space.

I think of England,
my island home.

Our lifeboat
is my island now.

And as
it becomes
harder to talk,
each of us
on the boat
becomes
an island
unto ourselves,
each of us alone
in a great sea
of silence.

## The Keys

We need our story
more than ever.
"We'll help you, Mary,"
I say.

"Bulldog and the boys
need to visit the pub,"
says Fred. "The Ship's Pub . . ."

"To find the keys," says Paul.

"Mary goes with Bulldog and the boys,
pretending they're a family," I say.

Mary wraps her arms
around our shoulders
and shares a weak smile
with Father O'Sullivan.

"We *are* a family, aren't we," she says.
She sits up
struggles to speak,
and goes on . . .

The family went to the pub for lunch. Cage, the
owner, came out of the kitchen and asked what
they'd like to order.

"Fish and chips," I say.

"Bangers and mash," says Fred.

"Chicken," says Derek.

"Ice cream," says Billy.

Bulldog asked to use the telephone while the
others ordered. He looked around the room.
Keys, where would they find a set of keys?

"What kind of keys?"
asks Derek.
"Automobile keys? House keys?
Keys to a safe?"

I look at Mary
and have an idea:

Ken tapped Bulldog on the shoulder
and pointed to the piano in the corner
of the room.

"The piano," says Mary.
"Ah, brilliant, my boy.
I can just see
my piano at home."

The thought of her piano

makes her sit up a bit.
She stares at her hands,
taps her fingers,
and begins again.

The keys were piano keys. But which ones?
Bulldog nodded to Mary and she walked over
to the piano.

*"Oi!"* yelled Cage. "That piano is broken. Don't
touch it!"

Bulldog held him back as Mary stared down at
the keys and thought about the kidnapped pilots.
They were being held prisoner somewhere.
But where? She glanced at the owner. Ah!

She played the keys C ... A ... G ... E.

Nothing happened.

She thought again of those flying aces and
stared at the notes on the keyboard. She played
three more notes: A ... C ... E.

Nothing happened except Cage lunged to stop
her. Bulldog held him in a firm grip.

"You're on to something, Mary," said Bulldog.
Then his gaze fell on four pictures hanging on

the back wall. Inside each was a framed playing card: an ace of hearts, diamonds, clubs, and spades.

"Interesting artwork," said Bulldog.
"Four aces.
Four ace pilots.
Play that again, Mary. Play A . . . C . . . E. Play it four times."

And Mary did as Cage thrashed.
This time a secret door in the back wall slid open.
What was inside?

"The four aces!" we all shout.

"Right, you are," said Mary.

The boys freed the pilots and Bulldog hustled Cage off to the police. Peterson's plan to sell the codes was foiled and thanks to those pilots, England wins the war. Another Bulldog Drummond case closed, all thanks to those marvelous boys.

The End

"But wait, Mary!" I say.
"What happened to Peterson?

Did he die in the fire?
Did he get away?"

Mary smiles weakly,
closes her eyes,
and says,
"That, my dears,
is a story
for another day."

## The End

The story
that was keeping us alive
                              is over.

We are all too weak to begin another.

All that's left is a boundless ocean,
            a bottomless thirst. . . .
            Hope of rescue is a small buoy left behind
                        as each wave
                  pushes us toward our unhappy end.

## I Wonder

Lying back,
I stare
up to the blue. . . .

We saved the pilots,
but where is Peterson?
Is evil alive
      in a U-boat?
         In a bomber?

Our water is almost gone.

I stare
up to the cloudless sky,
up to heaven.

My mum is there,
the one I never knew,
my mum who died
when I was just a baby.

I wonder
what is it like up there,
to float up there,
to stay up there forever
with my mum. . . .

## Out of the Blue

I blink.
There's a speck in my eye.
NO!
It's a speck in the sky
growing
bigger,
blacker,
brighter.

I sit up,
stand up,
and point.
"Look, an airplane!" I shout.

"It's a plane,
    a plane,
       a PLANE!"

Everyone stares at me
and looks where I'm pointing.
They don't believe me.

    "It can't be."
        "It's just a seagull."
"It's just a cloud."
        "It's just a mirage."

We've seen gulls and clouds and smoke and ships before.

They all vanished,
               wisps in the wind.

But this time I know!

"NO, I tell you! It's a plane."

I pull off my pajama top and use it
to wave and wave and wave.

        IT'S A PLANE!!!


## A German Plane?

"Ken's right," cries Cooper. "It's a plane!"
"Everyone down!"

WHAT? What is he *doing*?

"It could be a German plane. We don't know."

"I know!"
I've read about it
a million times.
I traced its shape
and memorized its name
and the sound of its engines.

"It's a Sunderland—
a Flying Boat."

## On Our Feet

Now they believe me.
Everyone is standing,
calling, waving,
flashing our milk tins
in the sun.
But will it see us?

"Boys, we must pray," says Father O'Sullivan.
"We must pray harder than ever."

The sailors continue to shout and wave,
but I pray like I've never prayed before.
"We pray that the plane will come
close enough to see us, and bring us help."
It is almost too much to hope.
But we saved the pilots with Bulldog,
                                    remember?
And now this pilot will save us.
"Please, God, hear our prayer.
Please, God, let that pilot see us. . . ."

## And He Does

The plane drops down.
We hear its drone.

We spot the British roundels
as the wings pass overhead.

It IS a Sunderland!

The pilot zooms down,
swoops around,
and WAVES!
Oh, heaven,
he's seen us!

"HE'S COMING!" I shout.
"He is, my boy, he is," says Cooper.
The officers whoop and
the crewmen point and shout at the sky.

Signalman Mayhew
says, "We need flags!"
Buxoo shouts to some of his men,
who quickly unwind their turbans.

Mayhew stands,
holding his makeshift flags,
out,
down,

right,
up,
overhead,
left.

It's a code.
I learned the signals
in the Army Cadets
last year when I was twelve—
each stance spells
a letter of the alphabet:

C
I
T
Y

Slowly the words come together:
C-I-T-Y
O-F
B-E-N-A-R-E-S.

The plane circles two, three times.
Its Aldis lamp
flashes a code.

"Lower the sail," says Cooper.

Mary looks up and asks,
"Am I dreaming?"

"It's no dream, Auntie Mary!"
I say. "We are saved!"

*Clang! Clang! Clang!*
We boys grab our milk tins,
banging them together
noisemakers,
merrymakers.
We're giddy
with hilarity and hugs.

"Oh boy," cries Howard.
"We're going to fly home!"

"Thanks be to God,"
says Father, who reaches up to heaven
and then lays a hand on
each of our heads,
blessing us all.


## Too Rough to Land

The pilot's lamp
winks and blinks a message:
low on fuel,
radioing for help,
dropping food.

*Splash!*
There it is!
But the bag of food
falls too far from us
and is swept away.

The plane soars off,
growing smaller
and smaller
as it flies east.

Then it's gone.
"WAIT!" Derek shouts.
"Come back!" yells Fred.

"It's all right!" I say.
"He's getting help."

I have a question,
but I keep it to myself.
How will they ever find us again?


## Limbo

The minutes tick by
as we continue
to search the sky.

Five minutes,

ten,
fifteen,
but there! Listen!
A hum thrums above.
A second plane
appears to cheers!
It drops a parachute bag
attached to a life preserver
to keep it afloat.

This time,
it lands a few feet away.
Inside are flares
and a feast of canned peaches and pears,
soups, fish, and beans.

Still no water,
but we open the cans
and suck down the fruit juices
and other liquids inside.

Best of all,
there's a handwritten note:
"Rescue vessel
40 miles away."

A ship—

A SHIP—

is coming!

## At Last

At 4:30 pm
on Wednesday, September 25,
Day 8—
the day our water would run out—
the Royal Navy has come for us.

At last.

Mayhew fires off the flares
the plane dropped
as the ship pulls into view.
We wave and wave and wave
and toast each other
with the last of our water.

As the ship approaches,
I grin at my Indian friend
and yell, "Huzzah!"

He looks at me quizzically
and repeats, "Huzzah?"

I point to the ship. "Huzzah!"
He looks and says, "Ah, *Hurrē!*"
"*Hurrē!*" I shout.

Then, in the dazzling sun,
the A-class destroyer

HMS *Anthony*—
Anthony,
the name of the patron saint
of the lost—
pulls up by our side.
We are safe.

Safe at last.

RESCUE

## Salvation

We work the Fleming gear
to row the short distance
to the ship.
"Ahoy, young mates!"
say the grinning sailors.
They toss nets
over the side of the ship
and say, "Right! Up you come."

I can't move!
My muscles and joints
are too weak.
The sailors scramble down
and hoist us boys up
above their shoulders.
Others lean down to pull us
onto the destroyer.

## Sick Bay

On deck,
I hobble,
just like the others,
suffering
from trench foot

and frostbite.
Paul can't walk at all,
his legs are really gone.

It's a little terrifying
to realize I can't walk,
let alone run as I used to.
Still a boy of thirteen,
I limp like an old man,
an ancient mariner. . . .

The sailors speak in hushed tones
as they usher us
into the sick bay.
I hear one doctor say
none have suffered more
than the crew:
"Fingers and toes came off
in the dressings."

Still, we are alive.


## Doctor's Orders

"You'll be all right, boys,"
says the doctor,
examining me with the others.
"Just give it a little time."

"When can we eat, sir?" asks Fred.

"No solid food for now," he says.
"Liquids are what you need."
He gives us water
and a little thin gruel.

"Come with us, chaps," say the sailors.
They help us below deck
to take warm baths
and towel ourselves dry.
One picks up my wet,
salt-encrusted pajamas.
"Out with these!" he says.

"Don't throw out my overcoat!
I promised my mum
I'd take care of it."

The sailor shakes his head and smiles.
"Very well, but put these on," he says,
offering me one of his uniforms instead.
It's much too big.

I laugh when I see my friends again—
we're a funny lot,
in saggy, baggy sailor suits
with the legs and sleeves rolled up.

"Hats off to you, boys!" says one sailor,

giving me his cap.
His friends hoist us up
on their shoulders,
jolly us up
on piggyback rides
all around the ship,
to the engine room,
the gun deck,
up, down, and everywhere.
They make us feel like royalty.
There is nothing they don't do for us.

"To the mess hall!" shouts one,
and we parade inside
where we disobey doctor's orders.

"Here, Ken, try this," says one,
feeding me soft fruit—
lush spoonfuls of
peaches, pears, and apricots,
all covered in cream,
sweet, silky mouthfuls.
I can't get enough.

But it's too much.
"Where is the loo?" I ask in a hurry.

"I've got to go too!" says Derek.
We're nipping off
to the toilets again,
right as rain.

# THURSDAY, 26 SEPTEMBER

## Real Food

The next day the doctor says
we can eat again.
Real, honest-to-goodness food.
I've never had sandwiches so thick—
a tin of salmon between two slices of bread
an inch wide. Gorgeous!
And hot sweet tea to revive us.

## Lucky 13

It's early evening
when HMS *Anthony*
steams into Princes Pier,
Gourock, Scotland.
We line the ship's rails,
waving to throngs
of weeping people
and press who have come to greet us.

"Remember the day we shipped out?" asks Derek.

I think of leaving Liverpool
a lifetime ago,
then realize something with a shock.
"It was just thirteen days ago."

"And here we are,
back on dry land,"
says Derek.
"See, I told you!
Thirteen IS our lucky number!"

Horns blow
and sailors scramble with lines
as the ship slips up to the dock.
On shore people press against the ropes,
cheering and waving.
Flashbulbs pop!
I feel stage fright,
but the sailors behind us
pat our backs
and adjust our caps.

"Smile, boys!" they say.
"Smile for the newsreels!"
I can't help but grin
in my super-sized
sailor suit and cap.
My friends and I wave and wave
to the crowds,
giving two thumbs-up.

The gangplanks are lowered
and we get ready to hobble off the ship.

The sailors will have none of it!
They hoist us up,
triumphant survivors
riding piggyback
on Royal Navy shoulders.

So many eyes staring at us,
so many hands pointing,
so many beaming faces.
I feel my cheeks flush,
but it's thrilling all the same.
So many cheers,
all for us!

A throng of reporters
press in,
but make way when Paul
is carried off the ship
on a stretcher,
swaddled in blankets
up to his chin.

I stare at the pain
on his face,
at his panicky eyes
darting about.
"Paul, you'll be all right,"

I shout. "They'll fix you up
in no time."

Paul smiles weakly
as they hurry him
into the waiting ambulance
and off to hospital.

A nearby reporter
catches my arm and says,
"Congratulations, young man.
You boys sure are the lucky ones!"

Someone in the crowd shouts
and holds up a newspaper.
"Look! You're front-page news!"

There it is—our story
in the headlines:
BACK FROM THE DEAD!
THOUSAND-TO-ONE CHANCE
COMES OFF IN MID-ATLANTIC,
says *The News of the World*.

Thousand-to-one chance,
and yes, I'm a lucky one.

# Bombed at Home or Torpedoed at Sea?

Reporters step up
to pepper us with questions.
"How do you feel
about coming home to the war?"
asks one reporter.
It's our old game:
Bombed at home or torpedoed at sea?
Silly man. The game has changed.
I tell him,
"It doesn't matter about the bombs falling.
We are no longer COLD.
There's nothing worse than being
wet and cold and not being able to get warm."

"What's the first thing
you'd like for supper on land?"
asks another reporter.
I know for sure.
"Ice cream and fish and chips."

"There will be plenty of time
for questions later," says an official,
pushing the press aside.
"What these boys need is supper and a bed!"

## A Real Bed

We are whisked off to a meal
and beds in a Glasgow hotel.

After supper, I change into
cozy pajamas,
fingers trembling a little
as I button them up.

I climb into a great, still, pillowy bed
and stare at the ceiling for hours.

Who can sleep?
This bed doesn't rock
and it's entirely
too warm
      too dry
         too soft.

## Fame and a Fortune

First thing,
my friends and I are taken
to a reception in our honor
hosted by the Glasgow Lord Provost.

It goes by in a blur
of speeches and tears
and gifts of coats,
badges, gold brooches,
and keys to the city.

It's fun being fussed over,
but deep down
I can't help feeling like an imposter.
It's not like we did anything special
to deserve all of this.

All we did was hang on.
Survive.

But there's no stopping

the ceremonies
and the parade of gifts.
Being in Scotland,
they give us kilts.
"Choose any clan you like!" they say.
I choose Hunting Gordon—
darkish green
with a yellowish stripe.
I'll give it to my sister
when I get home.
It's not likely I'll wear it
once I get back to London, is it?

When WILL they let us get home?
And after that, what?
Will we try again,
set off on another ship for Canada?
I can't think about that now.

The Glasgow Lord Provost
leads us to his library.
"I would like to give each of you a book,"
he says. "Choose whichever one you like."

Ah! Now there's a gift I'll take.
Which book do I choose?
Adventure stories, of course!

In the afternoon,
Mr. Nagorski keeps his promise.

He replaces our pocket money.
And then he doubles it.

We knew he was a millionaire.

## Questions

Later, Red Cross workers tend to us
and try to answer our questions.

"What happened after the ship sank?" I ask.
"What happened to the others from the *Benares*?"

"Oh, you don't know, do you?" says one.
"A rescue ship—HMS *Hurricane*—
found them the day after the *Benares* sank.
They pulled survivors from the water
and brought them home. They're safe!"

SAFE! They're safe!

"Where's my friend Terry?" I ask. "Terrence Holmes.
Is he back home now? I can't wait to see him!"

"And where's my little brother, Alan?" asks Derek.
         "An' mine?" asks Billy. "His name is Peter."

"Let's see," they say. "We can look them up."
The Red Cross workers consult their paperwork,

running their fingers
down the ship's list of names.
"Terrence Holmes? Here.
Ah, let's look up Alan Capel.
And how about Peter Short?"
They exchange glances.

"What? What is it?" I say.

They sit us down to give us answers
we don't want to hear.

Not one of them survived.
Not Terry. Not Alan. Not Peter.

Billy and Derek start to cry,
but I can barely hear
with the noise in my head.
Pictures rewind
of Terry pulling me into shelters,
picking up shrapnel,
drawing his ships,
laughing at my jokes,
kicking a football,
racing go-carts.
"Ken!" he calls.
"Ken Sparks! Canada, here we come!"
Terry will never see Canada.
And I will never see my friend
                                    again.

Only thirteen children
from our original ninety
are still alive.

Thirteen.

## Writing Home

Telegrams go out
to our parents:

DELIGHTED CONFIRM OFFICIALLY THAT YOUR BOY
IS SAFE AND WELL LANDED GLASGOW. IF YOU WISH
TO FETCH HIM, THIRD CLASS RETURN FARE WILL BE
PAID. IF NOT, HE WILL BE ESCORTED BACK TO YOU
AS SOON AS POSSIBLE. PLEASE WIRE OR TELEPHONE
YOUR INTENTION. REJOICE AT SURVIVAL OF YOUR
GALLANT SON.

While we wait for our parents to fetch us,
Auntie Mary suggests we write letters home.
"Ken," says Mary,
reading over my shoulder.
"You didn't tell them that
YOU
were the one
who spotted that plane.
You are our hero."
I smile and feel my face flush,

but I don't say anything.

Mary touches my arm.
"They're going to be very proud of you,
my boy."

## Reunited

Billy's parents arrive first
and swoop him up in their arms.
Billy wraps his arms round his mum's neck
and hides his face in her shoulder
while his dad's arms encircle them both.
"Mummy," Billy says, choking.
"Mummy."

"Yes, Billy, I've got you."

"Mummy . . ."

"What is it, sweetheart?"

Billy takes a big hiccupping gulp.
"Mummy, I havenae got Peter for you."

"Billy, my Billy," she says,
tears streaming down her cheeks
as she wipes his away
and whispers in his ear.

"Oh, my darling, darling boy,
I still have you!"

Other parents appear soon after
and the tender scene plays over
and over again.
I stand to the side
watching the family reunions,
full of smiling tears
and talk of miracles.

"I had never given up hope,"
Fred's mum tells the others.
"Monday, Tuesday, and Wednesday
I dreamed that I saw him safe in a boat."

Howard's dad tells of three wardens at his door.
"I thought . . . we were being evacuated but
they said, 'We have good news.'
I answered, "You're going to tell me my boy
is alive," and they said, 'Yes!' "

Mrs. Shearing says,
"I can hardly believe the good news.
A miracle has happened."

Derek's mum gives her a hug.
"We thought we had lost both boys.
It's a miracle that Derek has been snatched
back from the grave."

A miracle, yes.
Found sons, joyful parents.
But where are mine?

## They're Not Coming

This morning
I receive a telegram:

KINDLY ESCORT HOME KENNETH SPARKS. IMPOSSIBLE
TO COME = SPARKS

I'm to make my way home
on my own.

I slump to the floor
and think of all I've been through.
Now I'm home,
but home hasn't changed.
Money is still tight.
My father can't leave work.
My stepmum feels the same.

"Ken, mate, come with us!"
says Howard.
"We can get you
down to Euston Station."

Home hasn't changed.
BUT
            I have.

The sea may have knocked me down
and left me for dead,
but this odd mix of kind people
thrown together on Lifeboat 12—
people who were once strangers—
started my heart again.
They nursed me back to myself,
stronger than ever.

I smile at my new friend Howard,
who gives me a hand up.
"Thanks, mate! That would be grand."


## Good-byes

Soon it's time
for us all to say good-bye,
but no one has the words.

Head down,
hands in pockets,
I stand on one leg,
then the other.
I stare at the floor,
hardly believing

I won't be seeing these chaps
tonight,
tomorrow,
and all the days
for the rest of my life.
They feel like family.

"We must be going," says one parent.
"Five more minutes."

I swallow and look up
at the others.
"I've always wanted . . . ," I say.

"What?" asks Derek.
I try again.

"I've always wanted a brother.
Now I have you lot."

"Come here, boys,"
says Auntie Mary,
and folds us in,
arm over arm.
"You'll see each other again,"
she says.
"You can write to each other.
And to me."

"We will," I say.

Parents gently pull their sons away.
Mrs. Claytor reaches for Howard and me.

"Just one more minute," I say.

"All right, dear," she says.
We'll wait for you in the hall."

I put out my hand to Father O'Sullivan.
"Good-bye, Father," I say.
"Thanks for taking care of us.
I'll . . . I'll try to pray more."

"Good-bye, Ken.
I'll pray that you do!"
He laughs, clasping my hand in both of his.
"And we'll be in touch.
Don't you worry!"

Lastly, I turn to Mary.
"Good-bye, Auntie Mary."

"Ken, dear heart,
I'm so proud of you.
You were very brave,"
she says, cupping my cheek
in her hand.

"I'll always remember your stories,
Auntie Mary."

"And I'll always remember *you*."
Then she gives me a kiss.

I turn to go.
"Make your way," my parents say.
And yes, I can do it now.

       I can make my way.

## Back in London

The train chugs into Euston Station.

I glance eagerly down the platform,
hoping for a familiar face.

No one.
No one has come to meet me.
It's okay.
I know my way home.

Then
I hear my name.
"KEN!"

It's my dad,
MY DAD!
I hobble as fast as I can
into his outstretched arms.
He hugs me hard
and try as I might,
I can't stop the blasted tears.

Harry Peard would be disgusted.
"What a lot of rot," he would say.

Dad laughs, wipes his own eyes and nose,
stares hard into my eyes,
and says, "I thought I'd lost you."

"I'm safe, Dad. I'm safe."

Arm in arm,
leaning on each other,
we make our way home.

Together.

## Homecoming

Back in Wembley,
I turn the corner
to Lancelot Crescent,
where a crowd lines the street!
The rest of my family
stands at the gate to our house,
flanked by people on either side
clapping and cheering
beneath Union Jack flags
hung from every window.

My little sister gives me a kiss.

"You've made us proud," says Mum.
The neighbors crowd in around us.

The mayor of Wembley
steps up. "Ken," he says,
"we took up a collection
to buy you a welcome home gift."

He hands me a small box.
"Open it."
I look at the smiling faces
and lift the lid.
Inside is a silver watch.
"There's an inscription,"
says the mayor.
"Read it."
I turn the watch over and read aloud:

PRESENTED TO KENNETH SPARKS
BY HIS NEIGHBORS IN ADMIRATION
OF HIS DAUNTLESS COURAGE
WHEN TORPEDOED IN
SS *CITY OF BENARES*
SEPTEMBER 17, 1940

Dad says to my stepmum,
"He's really home."

"Now we can look at his bike
without crying," she whispers.

Crying?
I look up at her in surprise
and, maybe for the first time,
notice how weary she looks.

I turn to see two houses across the street
have been bombed
and the sidewalks are full of rubble.
They've had a tough time of it here, too.

I turn back to hear what
my mum is saying.
"When we first heard
that the ship had gone down,"
she tells our neighbor,
"we read that boys
in one boat were heard singing
'Roll Out the Barrel.'
It's Kenny's favorite song,
and I knew he was in that boat.
I could see him standing up
and singing in his new grey overcoat.
Every time I thought about the singing,
it made me go on hoping."

Hoping? What?
She wipes a tear,
an honest-to-God tear.
For me.

I try to cheer her up.
"Look, Mum," I say.
"I still have my coat.
I went back to get it.
That's how I missed Lifeboat 8."

"Missed it for a coat? Oh, Ken!"
she says.

"Newspapers say Lifeboat 8
had no survivors,"
our neighbor says softly.

"I went back to get my coat," I say.
"That's how I ended up in Lifeboat 12."

"Oh!" Mum cries, covering her mouth.
Slowly she reaches a hand to me.

I reach right back.

## How to Survive

I was the boy
who shouldn't have been born.

But I was.

I was the boy
who shouldn't have survived.

But I did.

I was the boy
who spotted the plane
and, according to the newspapers,
"saved all of those lives."

They say I'm a hero.
I say I'm a survivor.

I survived thanks to
the kindness of
people I didn't know,

people who were all different,
people who wanted to help.

We've stayed in touch
these three years.
We always will.

The war rages on.
I know what I want to do.
All the boys
from Lifeboat 12
are doing the same.

We're going to help.


## A New Chapter

I stand in a long queue
staring up at a war poster
of Nazis burning books.
The caption reads,
"Books are Weapons in the War of Ideas."
I tuck my book under my arm.
No wonder the Nazis don't want people to have them.
For them, books are weapons.
For me, stories are lifesavers.

"Next!" says the man
at the desk.

Forms,
questions,
inspections.
They stamp my papers.
I sign my name.

"Welcome to the Royal Navy, young man."

I once thought the story of my life was over,
                    but it has just begun.

                    And I can make my way.

# AUTHOR'S NOTE

Dear Readers,

*Lifeboat 12* is based on a true World War II story I discovered in the teenage letters of my mother-in-law, Nancy Hurst-Brown Kueffner. Nancy was a British child evacuated just before the *Blitz*, thankfully on a different ship that did reach Canada. Once safely ashore, Nancy exchanged letters with her mother discussing news of the SS *Volendam*, which was torpedoed with 321 children aboard. Nancy wrote, "Isn't it marvelous that all the children were saved?" That certainly grabbed my attention and I had to read more. Researching that story led me to the SS *City of Benares*.

    The tragic events aboard the *Benares* and the miracle of Lifeboat 12's rescue are so astounding that my first thought was to write a nonfiction book. Otherwise, I feared no one would believe it! But I know how young readers like to get inside a character's head. In the end, I decided to write a hybrid book—part historical fiction (creatively retelling the facts from young Ken's point of view) and part nonfiction (using carefully documented information about the actual people, places, dates, and events).

In the summer of 1940, Hitler was at England's doorstep. France had surrendered weeks earlier in June and with Germans just across the English Channel, Englishmen worried that a full-scale invasion of their island was next. So when other countries offered to take British children, Parliament formed the Children's Overseas Reception Board (CORB) to ship them to safer shores. The program selected children (ages 5 through 15) by lottery and sent them off to Canada, Australia, New Zealand, and South Africa (the British Dominions). Children traveled without parents but with adult escorts (teachers, religious leaders, doctors, and nurses). Neither Winston Churchill nor Queen Elizabeth wholly approved; Parliament's decision seemed to signal that Britain was already on the run. Some had suggested the Queen evacuate with her daughters. She replied, "The children won't go without me. I won't leave the King. And the King will never leave."

Ken Sparks and his new friends were not the first to evacuate. The CORB program launched on June 20 and in ten days more than 211,000 children registered for 20,000 spots. Everyone was soon aware of the dangers. Near midnight on August 30, the SS *Volendam* with 321 children on board was torpedoed by a German U-boat 70 miles off the coast of Ireland. Only one of the two torpedoes exploded, so while the ship was gouged, it didn't sink. All but one of the 606 passengers disembarked into lifeboats and were rescued by British ships. The ship's purser was the only casualty. Two children, Patricia Allen and Michael Brooker, returned home to find their houses bombed, so they were squeezed onto the next trip on the *Benares*.

One week later, on September 7, 1940, the *Blitzkrieg*, or "Lightning War," began. Late that afternoon, London was attacked by 348 German bombers, escorted by 617 fighter planes; sky-high fires along the docks of the East End lit the way for another round of nighttime bombers. By daybreak, 430 men, women, and children had been killed and more than 1600 injured. The bombing continued for 57 consecutive nights. Given the choice of "bombed at home or torpedoed at sea," parents chose the lesser of two evils. They were assured that each evacuee ship would sail in a convoy under the protection of the Royal Navy.

Normally, seamen would delay an unlucky departure date of Friday the 13th, but there was no time to lose. So the SS *City of Benares* left Liverpool at 6:15 pm that day on her first Atlantic crossing. Crewed by 166 Asian crewmen and 43 European seamen, the ship sailed for Quebec and Montreal in a convoy of 18 ships, escorted by the destroyer HMS *Winchelsea* and two corvettes, and watched over at first by a Sunderland flying boat.

By Tuesday, September 17, the ship was 600 miles from shore. Typically, U-boats didn't venture that far offshore, so rules were relaxed. Escorts allowed children to remove their life jackets and change into pajamas for the first time. However, they hadn't taken one thing into account: Since the fall of France earlier that summer, U-boats were now based in French ports and could travel farther into the Atlantic than ever before.

That night, the *City of Benares* was torpedoed by a German *Unterseeboot*—U-boat 48. Official reports put the time at about 10:05 pm. The first two torpedoes missed, but the third hit the ship's no. 5 hold on the aft port side, one level below the children's cabins. Two children were killed instantly. Reports say there was no panic; passengers trained for just such an emergency and proceeded to their lifeboats in an orderly fashion.

The ship started to list to the port side and sink in the stern. Captain Landles Nicoll, 51, gave orders to abandon ship. Unfortunately, in high seas and force 10 (55 mile-an-hour) winds, many lifeboats flipped or swamped as they were lowered, especially those on the starboard side. Ken Sparks had been originally assigned to Lifeboat 8; it was among the first to be lowered on starboard. One end fell and the boat dangled vertically until a huge wave hit the boat, flinging more than 30 men, women, and children into the frigid sea. There were no survivors. If Ken had not gone back to get his coat, he would have been aboard.

As luck would have it, Ken boarded Lifeboat 12 instead. Farthest astern on the port side, Lifeboat 12 was the only boat lowered without incident and it took on little water. Fourth Officer Ronnie Cooper assumed command and directed the lifeboat away from the sinking ship. As noted by the U-boat commander, the *City of Benares* sank at 10:34 pm.

The *Benares'* SOS and position (56.43° North, 21.15° West) had been picked up in Scotland and relayed to the Naval Western Approaches in Liverpool. HMS *Hurricane*, under Lieutenant Commander Hugh Crofton Simms, was directed to proceed to the rescue "with the utmost dispatch." Simms knew immediately that meant women and children were involved. Traveling more than 300 miles, fighting heavy waves and a force 8 gale, the *Hurricane* arrived on the scene of the sinking around 2:30 pm the following day. Survivors had been in the water for sixteen hours. The *Hurricane*'s crew worked for four hours, rescuing 115 people, 105 from the *Benares*.

The rescuers knew to look for twelve lifeboats. Unfortunately, they mistakenly counted one of the two lifeboats from the *Marina*, the convoy ship that had been torpedoed four minutes after the *Benares*. Lifeboat 12 had drifted quickly out of the ship's searching pattern because it wasn't swamped with water. So while HMS *Hurricane* steamed back to Greenock, Scotland, Lifeboat 12 was left behind at sea.

The 30-foot* lifeboat spent eight days at sea, desperately sailing for Ireland with enough food for about three weeks and water for about eight days. Each person received about six ounces of water per day on the lifeboat, as opposed to the four quarts of water allocated to each person on the ship.**

The major events recounted aboard the lifeboat are based on actual events. Whales visited one day. A ship was spotted on the fifth day and it did indeed approach, only to turn away again; no one is quite sure why. Perhaps they

---

*Lifeboats on the *City of Benares* ranged in size from 23 to 30 feet.
** Scale of provisions, General Register and Record Office of Shipping & Seamen, Tower Hill, London, E.C.3. National Archives BT 381/1106.

suspected the lifeboat was a decoy, a ploy used by German U-boats to stop British ships within striking range and provide a stationary target for torpedoes.

Derek Capel's comment, "Thirteen is my lucky number," proved oddly prophetic. By a strange coincidence, the ship left on Friday the 13th in convoy OB213; Ken Sparks (the thirteen-year-old onboard) spotted the plane that saved them; they arrived back on land thirteen days after departure; and only 13 of the original 90 evacuee children survived. You just can't make this stuff up!

Ken Sparks was celebrated as "the boy who spotted the plane." It was a Sunderland, a seaplane from the Royal Australian Air Force that had been accompanying a convoy. It was headed back to England around 1:45 pm when the pilot, W. H. Garing, spotted a speck on the water. He couldn't be sure what it was and was about to fly off; then he spotted movement. It was Ken waving his pajama top!

Garing dove down for a closer look and saw a signalman spelling out C-I-T-Y-O-F-B-E-N-A-R-E-S by semaphore. But Garing was low on fuel.

He radioed a Royal Air Force Sunderland flown by Flight Lieutenant Doughie Baker. Baker zoomed over the lifeboat at about 2:00 pm, dropping food and a smoke float. Then he, in turn, radioed a ship two hours away and led it to Lifeboat 12.

At 4:30 pm, HMS *Anthony*, under Lieutenant Commander N. V. "Pugs" Thew, rescued Lifeboat 12 about halfway between the site of the sinking and the coast of Ireland (latitude 54.43° North/ longitude 14.20° West). They were still more than 300 miles from shore. After rescuing the passengers, they pulled the plug and Lifeboat 12 went to join the *Benares* at the bottom of the sea.

Lifeboat 12

As the *Anthony* steamed home, the telegrams went out to mourning parents, some of whom had already held funeral services for their children.

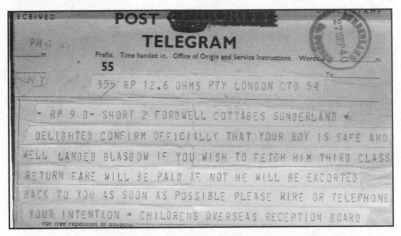

ECEIVED

PH 4

m

N T

**POST ~~PRIORITY~~**

**TELEGRAM**

27 SEP 40

Prefix. Time handed in. Office of Origin and Service Instructions. Words.

**55**

355 RP 12.6 OHMS PTY LONDON CTO 54

To

- RP 9 D- SHORT 2 FORDWELL COTTAGES SUNDERLAND -
DELIGHTED CONFIRM OFFICIALLY THAT YOUR BOY IS SAFE AND
WELL LANDED GLASGOW IF YOU WISH TO FETCH HIM THIRD CLASS
RETURN FARE WILL BE PAID IF NOT HE WILL BE EXCORTED
BACK TO YOU AS SOON AS POSSIBLE PLEASE WIRE OR TELEPHONE
YOUR INTENTION = CHILDRENS OVERSEAS RECEPTION BOARD

For free repetition of doubtful

Commander Thew sped the survivors to Gourock, Scotland, where, on September 26, they received heroes' welcomes.

From left to right: Ken Sparks, Derek Capel, Fred Steels, Howard Claytor, and Billy Short. Five of the six recued boys aboard the HMS *Anthony*. Note that Ken still has his overcoat.

*Dear Mum and Daddy*
*I hope you are all well and happy as you know that*
*I am safe we had a dreadful time on the lifeboat we*
*had very little water and a small piece of salmon or a*
*sardine on a ships biscuit we saw a huge whale and we*
*were ready to drive it away in case it broke the boat one*
*day we saw a boat which stopped for us but before we*
*were picked up it went away and we were disapponted*
*[sic] three days we floated around when we saw an*
*aeroplane which dropped us food and then went away*
*soon after two planes came along with a destroyer*
*which picked us up and we had good food and water.*

Ken's letter home to his parents. He modestly didn't mention his role in the rescue.

Mary Cornish, the only woman on Lifeboat 12, was lauded for her care of the boys. Her stories were based on Bulldog Drummond, a popular character in British books and movies that Ian Fleming credited as a model for his James Bond. King George VI awarded Mary the Order of the British Empire Medal in 1941, along with Ronnie Cooper and George Purvis.

Ramjam Buxoo was commended to the commander for his "unswerving devotion to duty assisting passengers at their boats and again during his 8 days in the No. 12 Lifeboat" and for "showing a very high standard of discipline which had a marked effect on the other native members of the crew."

Despite the happy ending for Lifeboat 12, the sinking of the *Benares* remains a horrific tragedy. Of the 406 passengers and crew, 253 people died in the water, including Billy Short's little brother Peter. Three children who were taken aboard HMS *Hurricane* unconscious did not survive the trip home: Ken's friend Terrence Holmes, Derek Capel's five-year-old brother Alan, and ten-year-old Derek Carr. Two crewmen, Ibrahim Balla and Abbas Bekim, died soon after they arrived back in Scotland.

Of the ninety evacuee children on board the *Benares* only thirteen survived in all, the six boys on Lifeboat 12 and seven others:

> Derek Alfred Capel (12)
> Henry (Howard) Francis Claytor (11)
> Paul Shearing (11)
> William (Billy) Cunningham Short (9)
> Kenneth John Sparks (13)
> Henry (Fred) Broderick Steels (11)
> John Baker (7)
> Elizabeth (Beth) Mary Cummings (14)
> Jack Sidney Keeley (8)
> Rex Ernest Thorne (13)
> Bessie Annie Walder (15)
> Louis Bernard Walder (10)
> Eleanor Wright (13)

In addition, seven children who were paying passengers survived, three of them remarkably from the same family.

The Children's Overseas Reception Board had successfully evacuated thousands of children: 1,532 to Canada, 576 to Australia, 353 to South Africa, and 203 to New Zealand. But as a result of the *Benares* tragedy, the CORB program was quickly canceled.

Importantly, the tragedy resulted in a major change in convoy policy. Starting in October 1940, convoys included a rescue ship, designated to stay and assist any damaged ships. This saved more than 4,194 lives in the coming years.

Five of the Lifeboat 12 boys grew up to join the Royal Navy. (Paul Shearing joined the Army instead.) Ken joined in 1944 as a boy bugler. When people spoke of him as a hero, he modestly told them, "We were *survivors*, not heroes."

Since then, *Bernares* survivors have held regular reunions. In 1988, according to a report in *The Independent*, they met two Germans who had been aboard U-boat 48: Wilhelm Kruse, the wireless operator, and Edouard Hansen, the engineer. Survivors of the *Benares* were "touched to hear that the German crew had been moved to tears on returning to their base in Lorient and discovering that the *Benares* cargo was mostly children."

# SOURCES

In my research, I consulted many primary sources at the National Archives, British Library, and National Maritime Museum in England, including firsthand accounts from survivors from both published and unpublished memoirs, recordings, newspaper articles, letters, ships' manifests, forms, telegrams, meeting minutes, and top secret government files that were only opened to the public in the 1970s. (See documented quotes on page 301.)

I read several Bulldog Drummond stories, but I concocted the story included here, weaving the boys' names into it, much the way Mary might have. All of the boys later said that it was Mary's stories that kept them alive.

I had the great good fortune to locate several of the "boys" of Lifeboat 12, now in their eighties or nineties, including Ken Sparks. I traveled to England in August 2015 and interviewed eighty-eight-year-old Ken, whose humor and optimism is reflected in a sign that hangs outside the small house where he has lived for forty years; it says: Shangri La. Ken was a lovely, funny, humble man with a great zest for life. He happily shared his story and a trunkful of memorabilia, including the silver watch he kept all these years. [See photo insert.] Tragically, Ken died two months later. This book is a tribute to him and all the other survivors.

# INTERVIEWS

Ken Sparks
Derek Capel
Derek Bech, a survivor whose family had been
    paying passengers
Blake Simms, son of Hugh Crofton Simms,
    commander of HMS *Hurricane*
Sean Hollands, nephew of Father O'Sullivan, and
    his wife Rosemary

# ADULT BOOKS

Barker, Ralph. *Children of the Benares: A War Crime and Its Victims.*
London: Grafton Books, 1990.

Balachandran, C. "Circulation through Seafaring: Indian Seamen,
1890–1945." In *Society and Circulation: Mobile People and Itinerant
Cultures in South Asia, 1750–1950.* Edited by Claude Markovits, Jacques
Pouchepadass, and Sanjay Subrahmanyam. London: Anthem Press, 2006.

Dixon, Conrad. "Lascars: The Forgotten Seamen." In *The Working Men
Who Got Wet.* Edited by R. Ommer and G. Panting. Newfoundland:
Memorial University Press, 1980.

Fethney, Michael. *The Absurd and the Brave: CORB—The True Account
of the British Government's World War II Evacuation of Children
Overseas.* Sussex: The Book Guild Ltd., 1990.

Fisher, Michael H.; Lahiri, Shompa; and Thandi, Shinder. *A South Asian
History of Britain: Four Centuries of Peoples from the Indian Sub-Continent.*
Oxford: Greenwood World Publishing, 2007.

Ghosh, Amitav. *A Sea of Poppies.* London: Picador, 2009

.

Huxley, Elspeth. *Atlantic Ordeal: The Story of Mary Cornish*. New York: Harper & Brothers, 1941.

Mann, Jessica. *Out of Harm's Way: The Wartime Evacuation of Children from Britain*. London: Headline, 2006.

Menzies, Janet. *Children of the Doomed Voyage*. Chichester, UK: John Wiley & Sons, Ltd. 2005.

Nagorski, Bohdan. "Eight Days in a Lifeboat." In *They Fight for Poland: The War in the First Person*. Edited by F. B. Czarnomski. London: George Allen and Unwin Ltd., 1941.

Nagorski, Tom. *Miracles on the Water: The Heroic Survivors of a World War II U-Boat Attack*. New York: Hyperion, 2006.

Panter-Downes, Mollie. *London War Notes 1939–1945*. New York: Farrar, Straus and Giroux, 1971.

Sapper (a.k.a. H. C. McNeile). *Bulldog Drummond: Premium 9 Book Collection*. Business and Leadership Publishing, 2014.

Smith, Lyn in association with the Imperial War Museum. *Young Voices: British Children Remember the Second World War*. London: Penguin, 2008.

Summers, Julie. *When the Children Came Home: Stories of Wartime Evacuees*. New York: Simon and Schuster, 2011.

Visram, Rozina. *Ayahs, Lascars and Princes: Indians in Britain 1700–1947*. London: Pluto Press, 1986.

Westall, Robert. *Children of the Blitz: Memories of Wartime Childhood*. New York: Viking, 1985.

## CHILDREN'S BOOKS

Lewis, Amanda West. *September 17*. Ontario: Red Deer Press, 2013.

# UNPUBLISHED MEMOIRS

O'Sullivan, Rory. *Join the Navy? Get Torpedoed First!*
Silver, Dorothy Perkins. *Rescued at Sea.*

# ORAL ACCOUNTS

Jack Keeley. June 28, 2000. Imperial War Museum
Ken Sparks. September 27, 2001. Imperial War Museum
Fred Steels. August 6, 2002. Imperial War Museum

# SONG CREDITS

Asaf, George, and Powell, Felix. "Pack Up Your Troubles in Your Old
Kit Bag and Smile, Smile, Smile." Lyrics © Warner/Chappell Music, Inc.,
Universal Music Publishing Group. London: 1915.

Parker, Ross, and Charles, Hughie. "There'll Always Be an England."
1939.

Thomson, James, and Mallet, David. "Rule, Britannia." 1740.

Vejvoda, Jaomír and Ingris, Eduard. "Roll Out the Barrel." 1927. English
lyrics by Lew Brown and Wladimir Timm. Also known as the "Beer Barrel
Polka." Lyicist Vaclav Zeman.

# PHOTO RESOURCES

SS *City of Benares*: Copyright Mersey Maritime Museum

Telegram: Courtesy of Kathleen Gill, Sunderland Volunteer Life Brigade

Photos of Ken and his family: Courtesy of Ken Sparks

Billy and Peter Short: Courtesy of Kathleen Gill, Sunderland Volunteer Life Brigade

Alan and Derek Capel: Courtesy of Ken Sparks

Cabin aboard the *City of Benares*: Courtesy of Kathleen Gill, Sunderland Volunteer Life Brigade

Children's playroom aboard the *Benares*: Courtesy of Kathleen Gill, Sunderland Volunteer Life Brigade

HMS *Hurricane*: Courtesy of Ken Sparks

Lifeboat 12: Copyright Associated Press

Father Rory O'Sullivan: Courtesy of Sean and Rosemary Hollands

Mary Cornish: Courtesy of Ken Sparks

Bohdan Nagorski, reunited with his daughters Barbara and Christine after the rescue: Courtesy of Tom Nagorski

Rescued boys aboard HMS *Anthony*: Copyright Associated Press

Ken's letter home: Copyright London Express News and Features
Ken's homecoming: Courtesy of Ken Sparks

Ken gets a kiss from his sis as the crowds welcome him home: Courtesy of Ken Sparks

Silver watch: Courtesy of Ken Sparks

Books Are Weapons in the War of Ideas poster: Copyright Getty Images

Eighty-eight-year-old Ken Sparks, 2015: Susan Hood

Note: The author has made every effort to secure permission to reprint photos and provide accurate copyright information. Other images were taken by the author or are believed to be in the public domain.

# INTERESTING WEBSITES

Additional photos: www.liverpoolblitz70.co.uk/2011/02/14/the-sinking-of-the-benares/

Bomb Sight: An interactive map that shows every bomb dropped on London during the *Blitz* from October 7, 1940 to June 6, 1941.bombsight.org

SS *City of Benares*: the Children's Ship. Merseyside Maritime Museum. http://www.liverpoolmuseums.org.uk/maritime/collections/city_of_benares

Burdette, J. G. "Destination Disaster: SS *City of Benares*." Web blog post. *Map of Time*. Wordpress, May 24, 2012. https://jgburdette.wordpress.com/2012/05/24/destination-disaster-ss-city-of-benares/

Partial list of crew and passengers aboard the *City of Benares* when the ship was hit. http://uboat.net/allies/merchants/crews/ship532.html

Info about Lascars and the East Indian Company in the Royal Museums Greenwich. http://www.rmg.co.uk/discover/explore/lascars-and-east-india-company

Report of interview with Fourth Officer, R. M. Cooper and crew casualty list. http://www.shipsnostalgia.com/guides/City_of_Benares_(survivors_report)%29

*City of Benares*: newspaper clippings and photos of the rescue. http://www.wrecksite.eu/wreck.aspx?57989

# VIDEOS

YouTube.com
 The First Day of the Blitz
 Amazing Archive footage and firsthand accounts

More *City of Benares* Survivors
Newsreel footage of the rescued boys, Mary Cornish, and Bohdan Nagorski. Paul Shearing, who suffered from trench foot, is taken off the ship on a stretcher.
Seavacuees Still Smiling
Footage of the children rescued by HMS *Hurricane* with remarks by Britain's King George IV.

# APPENDIX

SS *City of Benares*

A steam passenger ship built by Barclay, Curle & Co. Ltd., Glasgow, in 1936 for the Ellerman Line. At the time, it was the largest ship Ellerman had ever built. Typically, it sailed between India and England and got its name from Benares, a city in India, also known as Varanasi.

| | |
|---|---|
| Speed | 15 knots recommended speed |
| | 17 knots maximum speed |
| Gross Tonnage | 11,081 |
| Net Tonnage | 6,720 |
| Length | 486 feet, 1 inch |
| Beam | 62 feet, 7½ inches |
| Depth | 30 feet 8 inches |
| Official Number | 164096 |
| Code Letters | GZBW |

*Source: Lloyds Register, 1937/38 volume.*

# ABOARD LIFEBOAT 12

<u>Children</u>
Ken Sparks (13)
Derek Capel (12)
Howard Claytor (11)
Paul Shearing (11)
Fred Steels (11)
Billy Short (9)

<u>Escorts</u>
Mary Cornish (41)
Father Rory O'Sullivan (32)

<u>Paying Passenger</u>
Bohdan Nagorski (49)

<u>British Sailors</u>
Fourth Officer Ronnie Cooper (22)
Cadet Douglas Critchley (20)
Signalman Johnny Mayhew (19)
Gunner Harry Peard (38)
Assistant Steward George Purvis (23)

<u>Lascars</u>
Ramjam Buxoo
31 unnamed sailors

# ABOUT THE LASCARS

For hundreds of years, Asian sailors called Lascars were hired to work on European ships. By World War II, they made up a third of the British shipping industry. They "had nothing in common, except the Indian Ocean," according to author Amitav Ghosh. "Among them were Chinese and East Africans, Arabs and Malays, Bengalis and Goans, Tamils and Arakanese." Some were Hindu, some Muslim, and some (Goans) were Roman Catholic. They had different ethnicities and politics but were acclaimed for their bravery and seamanship. Ships' records offered little information about the Lascars. There was a language barrier to be sure. Also, Lascars were recruited in India by an agent called a *Ghaut Serang* and supervised onboard and in port by an Indian *serang* (boatswain). But the shocking lack of recordkeeping was also an indication of the racism of the time. The press was at fault, too. Newspaper accounts triumphantly detail the names, ages, and many life stories of the Europeans rescued. Yet after months of digging I was hard-pressed to uncover even a list of Lascars aboard Lifeboat 12. The only news item I could find was about the *Hurricane* rescue in the *Daily Express*. On September 23, 1940, it simply noted: "The saved include . . . thirty-six Lascar seamen." Ken Sparks said the Europeans and Indians were separated on the rescue ship and he never saw them again. He didn't know what happened to them.

Then one day, eureka! Hunting through documents in

the British Library, I came across the *Benares'* crew Injured List (dated October 7, 1940), which follows. I could find nothing to clarify whether these were men rescued by HMS *Hurricane* or picked up from Lifeboat 12 . . . or both. I was heartened to find Ramjan Buxoo [sic] , the man mentioned by several lifeboat survivors, listed here. Could the others be the men he cared for during those eight days?

## INJURED LIST

| | |
|---|---|
| Ebram Abdooramon | Second Tindal (Deck Storekeeper) |
| Essack Sk. Oomer | Lascar |
| Dawood Sk. Mahomad | Lascar |
| Ahmed Eusoof | Lascar |
| Kahomed Enoos | Lascar |
| Eusoofkhan Bapoo | Lascar |
| Hossein Ebrahim | Lascar |
| Sk. Esmail Sk. Adam | Lascar |
| Abdool Currim | Winchman |
| Sk. Allee Sk. Md. | Fireman |
| Sk. Allee Sk. Eusoof | Fireman |
| Hasson Mahomed | Fireman |
| Hasson Khan Alle Khan | Trimmer |
| Allum Terroo | Trimmer |
| Sultan Ali Hoosein | Trimmer |
| Abdul Rumjan | General Servant |
| Syfoo Mohamed Ali | Deck Steward |
| Abdul Ghafur Sk. Hiroo | Saloon Boy |
| Mohamdoo Futtey Khan | Saloon Boy |
| Shahzada Wahed Munshi | Bhandary's Mate (crew cook) |
| Sadeck Allee | Smokeroom Steward |

| Saizuddin Ebadat Mandal | Saloon Boy |
| Abdur Razzaque | Saloon Boy |
| Sheik Mathoo Sk. Sulaman | Saloon Boy |
| Lulla Bij Lall | Topas (sweeper or cleaner) |
| Sk. Habib Sk. Nawabjan | General Servant |
| **Ramjan Buxoo [sic]** | **General Servant** |
| Antonio P. Borges | Butcher |
| Ebrahim Abdul Rahim* | General Servant |
| Ebrahim Sk. Abdul** | Saloon Boy |

Note: These names were recorded phonetically by those in charge.

I checked Scotland's hospital records. The archivist for NHS Greater Glasgow & Clyde "could find no mention of Indian seamen being admitted in September/October of 1940." The records for the Greenock Royal Infirmary "are incomplete and the registers for 1940 have not been preserved."

All we know is that the numbers roughly add up:

166 Asian crewmen aboard the *Benares*

 – 101 casualties (names included on Ronnie Cooper's report)

= 65 survivors (number issued in final government report—
November 28, 1940

36 rescued by HMS *Hurricane*

+ 31 rescued by HMS *Anthony* (One man leapt overboard
before the rescue)

= 67 survivors

---

*Originally reported on both the casualty list and the injured list, but was crossed off the injured list.
**Ebrahim SK Abdul "should have been included on the injured list."—Superintendent, Registrar General of Shipping and Seamen. March 31, 1941.

Author Thomas Nagorski discovered two men who died of their injuries in early October: Ibrahim Balla and Abbas Bekim. Subtracting those two from 67, the number adds up to the government's final report of 65 Indian survivors issued on November 28, 1940.

Of these 65 lives, we know the names of 33 men. Sadly, even if the others had been listed on the *Benares'* manifest, that record went down with the ship.

# QUOTATION SOURCES

Documented quotes from interviews, oral accounts, and other sources are below.

p. 2 "... your preliminary application has been considered by the Board and they have decided that KENNETH J. SPARKS is ~~are~~ suitable for being sent to ... CANADA."  National Archives DO 131/91

p. 6 "And there will be a new overcoat ..."  Sparks interview
National Archives DO 131/91

"'penny cannon' fireworks."
"The Night We Were Torpedoed,"
*Observer Series*, January 23, 2003

p. 7 "a little so-and-so ..."  Sparks interview

"she wasn't supposed to have children."  Sparks interview

p. 8 "a clout round the ear hole or the cane at school."  Sparks interview

p. 16 "If it's going to hit us, it's going to hit us."  Sparks interview

p. 25 "German planes are diesel. They throb. Ours hum."  Sparks interview

p. 30 "She waves me good-bye, and that's it."  Menzies, p.17

p. 37 "It's just a bad habit."  Sparks interview

p. 39 "We're like seeds in a pod."  Nagorski, T., p. 27

p. 51    "No diseases must be allowed . . .
         to infiltrate the Dominion!"                    O'Sullivan, p. 21

p. 53    "The biggest thing we'd seen till then
         were the old paddle steamers in the Thames."    Sparks interview

p. 54    "Out of this world!
         And if it weren't for this . . . ,
         we'd never see anything like it."     Steels, Imperial War Museum

p. 57    44 boys to port, 44 girls to starboard

         Note: Sources disagree about this fact, but two eyewitnesses,
         Ken Sparks (later a Navy man) and Rory O'Sullivan, confirm
         this arrangement.

         "The girls to starboard, the boys to port . . ."    O'Sullivan, p. 22

         "boys on the port (left hand) side
         and girls on the
         starboard (right hand)."          Sparks account written as an adult

p. 60    "If you didn't make your own toys,
         you didn't get any."                            Sparks interview

p. 62    "It's a floating palace,
         is what it is!"                              Nagorski, T., p.35

         "three different kinds
         of knives and forks"                            Barker, p. 28

p. 63    "Fish and chips is my favorite."                Sparks interview

p. 66    "After the wartime food, . . .
         there aren't words to describe it.
         . . . We've never
         eaten so much in our lives."                    Menzies, p. 41

p. 86    . . . everything you could
         think of for a kid."                            Smith, p. 138

p. 88    "... the most magnificent
long cigarette holder [I've] ever seen!"          Menzies, p. 50

p. 89    "... pay their respects to the sea,
a bit green round the gills,
but ready to take on more ballast!"          O'Sullivan, p. 23

"... it's a Christmas dinner
every meal."          Nagorski, T., p. 47

p. 90    "Here, on this route, the first two days
may contain an element of danger,
but afterwards we should be quite all right."  Nagorski, B., p. 199

p. 98    "Blimey, if I go home without that coat,
[Mum] will kill me."          Sparks interview

p. 100   "The hatches have been blown off,
the emergency lights are on.
Electrical sparks ..."          Sparks, IWM

p. 104   "It's all right,
it's only a torpedo."          Huxley, p. 27

p. 105   "... like monkeys."          Sparks, IWM

p. 114   "... like a Christmas tree ..."          Menzies, p. 100

p. 117   "... went to its own grave."          Sparks, IWM

p. 129   "He looks like a duck,
coming out of its hole."          Nagorski, T., p. 209

"thirty feet of timber,
shorter than a London bus."          Fethney, p. 141

p. 133   "Water, water, everywhere
Nor any drop to drink."          "The Rime of the Ancient Mariner"
by Samuel Taylor Coleridge, 1798

p. 139    "One of the wheels had buckled
          so [someone] chucked it.
          Dad said, 'Here, you can mend that.'
          And I did. . . ."                          Sparks interview

          "I made a go-cart
          out of old pram wheels.
          . . . the rag-and-bone man."                Sparks interview

p. 145    "I was over the moon . . .
          [My Mum] kept hanging on to me.
          It was like trying to get away
          from an octopus. . . .
          Even [my Dad]
          had a few tears in his eyes.
          But . . . I couldn't wait. . . .."          Menzies, p. 14

          "One of my great-grandmothers
          ran off with a Jewish sailor, I think."      Capel interview

p. 146    "He sleeps through anything."               Nagorski, T., p.4

p. 149    "Why are you going swimming, mister?
          "To keep in practice,
          in case we get torpedoed again."            Barker, p. 187

          ". . . a proper screwball"                   Menzies, p. 164
          "Come on in, lads"                           Nagorski, T., p. 202
          "I love swimming!"                           Sparks interview
          "Ignore the man."                            Nagorski, T., p. 202

p. 150    "Now my wife,
          she's got a way with kids, she has.
          Keeps 'em fit as fleas,
          and stands no nonsense, neither.             Huxley, p. 58

What do you know about kids?
Got none of your own,
nor likely to have, either."

"You're right on both counts.
And what of it?"

p. 151    "No offense, of course."                    Huxley, p. 59

"What's the use of worrying,
it never was worthwhile.
So, pack up your troubles in your old kit bag,
and smile, smile, smile."
                                          Song credit on p. 302

p. 154    "sardines.
Yech!"                                      Sparks interview

p. 155    "Allah the Compassionate
was wise
and would send storms
if He thought best."                    Nagorski, T., p. 214

p. 159    If we aren't going
to be picked up one way,
we are going to get to Ireland.
Nobody has the slightest intention
of ever giving up hope.  No.              Sparks, IWM

p. 161    "Without a lie,
you could have put
two double-decker buses
in it!"                                      Smith, p. 140

"I shared a bunk bed
with Alan at home.
"I'd read to him
and he would read back to me.
He could tie his shoelaces
and he's only five."                      Capel interview

p. 166   "... water in a carafe,
         changed every day?
         I remember trying the water
         and it was so good,
         nice chilled water."                              Menzies, p. 40

p. 172   "Don't you realise
         that you're the heroes
         of a real adventure story?

         There isn't a boy in England
         who wouldn't give his eyes
         to be in your shoes!

         Did you ever hear of a hero who snivelled?"       Huxley, p. 54

p. 176   "I reckon you could ...
         mend the boat with them if you got holed."        Menzies, p. 157

p. 177   "... how we eye
         the water ration! ...                             O'Sullivan, p. 30

p. 178   "They must be frozen to death."                   Sparks, IWM

p. 179   "They weren't expecting
         to come out toward the Atlantic."                 Sparks, IWM

         "They're used to a hot country
         and the cold North Atlantic
         isn't anybody's fun."                             Menzies, p. 164

p. 186   "... as if to say
         what are *you* doing here
         in my waters?"                                    Sparks interview

p. 193   "It's like candy, is what it is. . . ."           Nagorski, T., p. 238

p. 201   "What's the matter now?"
         Down-'earted 'cos she didn't pick us up?
         *That's* nothing to worry about.

We'll see plenty more ships tomorrow,
now we've reached the sea lanes."                    Huxley, p.68

p. 220   "Drink . . .
         give me a drink . . .
         I am going mad!"                            O'Sullivan, p. 35

p. 221   *"il va mourir . . ."*                      Nagorski, T., p. 257

p. 222   "Water? Is *that* all?
         Of course you want water.
         We all do.
         You'll get your water in the morning!
         Now you forget about it.
         Is *that* all that's wrong with you?"       Huxley, p. 75

         "My feet are cold."                         Huxley, p. 198

p. 233   "a speck in the sky . . ."    *Yorkshire Post,* September 27, 1940

         "Look, an aeroplane!"                       Ibib

p. 235   "It's a Sunderland—
         a Flying Boat."                             Sparks interview

         "We pray that the plane will come
         close enough to see us, and bring us help."
         . . . too much to hope.          *Daily Mirror,* Sept 27, 1940

         "Please God, let that pilot see us . . ."   Nagorski, T., p.266

p. 237   "I learned the signals
         in the Army Cadets. . . ."                  Sparks interview

p. 238   "Oh boy!"
         "We're going to fly home!"                  Nagorski, T., p. 267

p. 242   "Safe at last."                             Sparks, IWM

p. 246   "Paul can't walk at all,
         his legs had really gone."                     Menzies, p. 169

         "fingers and toes came off
         in the dressings. . . ."                        Johnson, p. 115

p. 248   ". . . like royalty.
         There is nothing they don't do for us."          Sparks, IWM

p. 249   "I've never had sandwiches so thick—
         a tin of salmon between two slices of bread
         an inch wide. Gorgeous!
         And hot sweet tea to revive us."                   Smith, p. 153

p. 253   "It doesn't matter about the bombs falling.
         We are no longer COLD."                            Smith, p. 153

         "There's nothing worse than being
         wet and cold and not being able to get warm."      Sparks, IWM

         "Ice cream and fish and chips!"     *Daily Express,* Sept 27, 1940

p. 256   ". . . Hunting Gordon—
         darkish green
         with a yellow-ish stripe…"
         . . . not "likely I'll wear it
         once I get back to London, is it?"                 Sparks, IWM

p. 259   "DELIGHTED CONFIRM OFFICIALLY THAT YOUR BOY IS
         SAFE AND WELL LANDED GLASGOW. IF YOU WISH TO
         FETCH HIM THIRD CLASS RETURN FARE WILL BE PAID. IF
         NOT, HE WILL BE ESCORTED BACK TO YOU AS SOON AS
         POSSIBLE. PLEASE WIRE OR TELEPHONE YOUR INTENTION.
         REJOICE AT SURVIVAL OF YOUR GALLANT SON."

                              National Archives DO 131/20

p. 260   "Mummy, I have not got Peter for you"       Nagorski, T., p. 286

p. 261   "Monday, Tuesday and Wednesday
I dreamed that I saw him safe in a boat."
*Montreal Daily Star,* September 27, 1940

"I thought . . .
we were being evacuated but
they said, 'We have good news.'
I answered, "You're going to tell me my boy
is alive,' and they said, 'Yes!'" *Daily Express* September 28, 1940

"A miracle has happened."
*Montreal Daily Star,* September 27, 1940

"We thought we had lost both boys.
It's a miracle that Derek has been snatched
back from the grave."              Nagorski, T., p. 286

p. 263   "KINDLY ESCORT HOME KENNETH SPARKS.
IMPOSSIBLE TO COME = SPARKS"
National Archives DO 131/91

p. 270   Presented to Kenneth Sparks
By his neighbors in admiration
Of his dauntless courage
When torpedoed in
S.S. City of Benares
September 17, 1940

Sparks interview
*The Daily Mirror,* December 4, 1940

"Now we can look at [his bike]
without crying"
*Daily Express,* September 28, 1940

p. 271   "When we first heard
that the ship had gone down,
we read that boys
in one boat were heard singing

'Roll Out the Barrel.'
It's Kenny's favorite song,
and I knew he was in that boat.
I could see him standing up
and singing in his new grey overcoat.
Every time I thought about the singing,
it made me go on hoping."

*Daily Express*, September 28, 1940

p. 279    "The children won't go without me.
I won't leave the King. And the King
will never leave."

http://bmsf.org.uk/buckingham-palace-at-war/

p. 286    "unswerving devotion to duty
assisting passengers at their boats
and again during his 8 days in the
No. 12 Lifeboat."

"showing a very high standard of
discipline which had a marked effect
on the other native members of the crew. "

Letter to Commander, Holbrook, October 14, 1940
University of Glasgow Archives GB248 UGD, 131/1/37/208

p. 288    "We were *survivors*, not heroes."    Smith, p. 154

"touched to hear that the German crew
had been moved to tears on returning to
their base in Lorient and discovering that
the *Benares* cargo was mostly children."

Blake Simms in *The Independent*, September 17, 2010

p. 297    "had nothing in common, except the Indian Ocean,"
"Among them were Chinese and East Africans, Arabs
and Malays, Bengalis and Goans, Tamils and Arakanese."

Ghosh, p. 13

"The saved include . . . thirty-six Lascar seamen."
*Daily Express,* September 23, 1940


p. 299    "could find no mention of Indian seamen being
admitted in September/October of 1940."
records "are incomplete and the registers for 1940
have not been preserved."
NHS Greater Glasgow & Clyde archivist

# ACKNOWLEDGMENTS

I'm indebted to so many generous people for sharing contacts, doing research, answering my questions, clarifying facts. First on my thank-you list is Ken Sparks, who invited me to his home for several interviews and who shared his family photographs and trunk of memorabilia. Special thanks to Ken's son Robert Sparks, for answering my follow-up questions after his father's death.

Much gratitude to Tom Nagorski, great-nephew of survivor Bohdan Nagorski and author of a wonderful adult book about the *Benares* entitled *Miracles on the Water: The Heroic Survivors of a World War II U-Boat Attack*. Tom invited me to his home and shared some of his research and primary sources.

I am also greatly indebted to *Benares* survivors Derek Bech and Derek Capel; Sean Hollands (nephew of Rory O'Sullivan) and his wife Rosemary; Blake Simms (son of HMS *Hurricane* Lieutenant Commander Hugh Crofton Simms), Jim Perrin (who helped organize *Benares* reunions); Andrew Choong Han Lin (Curator, National Maritime Museum); Reverend Joseph F. Chorpenning, OSFS, S.T.L., Ph.D. (Editorial Director, Saint Joseph's University Press); Dorian Leveque (APAC Reference Services, British Library), Claire Daniel (Duty Archivist, University of Glasgow); Kathleen Gill (Deputy Head of Museum, Sunderland Volunteer Life Brigade); Dr. Alistair Tough (Archivist, National Health Service Greater Glasgow and Clyde); Dominic Blake

(BBC reporter); Dr. Shompa Lahiri (Research Fellow, Centre for the Study of Migration at Queen Mary University of London, and on the Diaspora Cities Project); and Dr. Ceri-Anne Fidler Jones (Lascar researcher).

Love and appreciation to friends Andrea Azarm, Jim Harman, and Laura Wilbur for their expertise; to author Patricia Reilly Giff, who encouraged and inspired me to write my first middle grade novel; to fellow authors who reviewed the manuscript—Eve Catarevas, Karen Jordan, Michaela MacColl, Carolyn Malkin, Page McBrier, Susan Montanari, Tracy Newman, and MaryJo Scott: to librarian Amy Hand; to my agent Brenda Bowen for calling me five minutes after she read my proposal; to my editors Christian Trimmer and Krista Vitola for taking a chance on a first-time middle grade author; Greg Stadnyk; to cousins David, Jackie, Tim, and Katie Hurst-Brown for lodging in England while doing research and for ensuring my British lingo was up to snuff; to my daughters Emily and Allison; and especially to my husband Paul Kueffner for his maritime smarts, his patience in listening to endless drafts, and his loving support.

PHOTOGRAPHS

Ken (right) with his sister Margaret and his father Charles

Ken (right) showed an early interest in ships and the sea

Ken Sparks, "full of beans"

Ken's mother Annie Harmes Sparks, who died when he was a baby

Ken with his sister Margaret and his stepmum Nora

Billy and Peter Short

Alan and Derek Capel

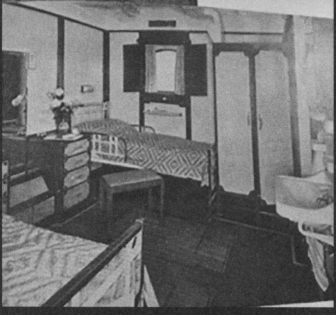

Cabin aboard the *Benares*

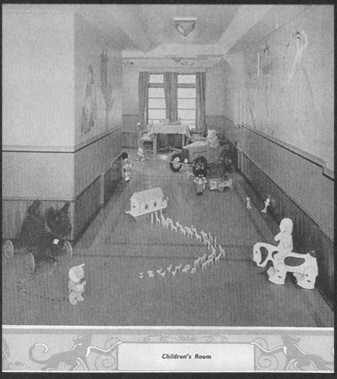

Children's Room

Children's playroom aboard the *Benares*

HMS *Hurricane* rescued survivors of the *Benares* on September 18, 1940

Father Rory O'Sullivan

Mary Cornish

Ken's homecoming

Ken gets a kiss from his sis as the crowds welcome him home

Bohdan Nagorski, reunited with his daughters
Barbara and Christine after the rescue

**Books cannot be killed by fire.**

People die, but books never die. No man and no force can put thought in a concentration camp forever. No man and no force can take from the world the books that embody man's eternal fight against tyranny. In this war, we know, books are weapons.

*Franklin D. Roosevelt*

## BOOKS ARE WEAPONS IN THE WAR OF IDEAS

This U.S. war poster is typical of ones Ken might have seen. During WWII, Nazis were burning books to stop the free flow of ideas. For Ken, his plane spotter book and Mary's stories were literally lifesavers.

Eighty-eight-year-old Ken Sparks, August 2015